Advance prai

'An exceptionally timely book, with a hugely appealing heroine in Isabella. Joan Lingard has enormous talent for bringing to life the tensions of families under pressure, and the pain of divided loyalties. She tells a serious story with a light touch and great warmth.' Lydia Syson, author of *A World Between Us* and *That Burning Summer*.

perfect example of how I think historical fiction should be done. It is ngaging, fast paced and historically accurate, doing justice to the times nd people involved.' Kirsty Connor, *The Overflowing Library*

hough I cannot seem to find adequate words to describe this book, know for certain that I fell in love with it. It's a quick read, and mpossible to put down, with engaging characters that have large ersonalities.' Ellie, Year 9 History student.

'A great story with a real connection with history and a very touching nd deep storyline. Joan is a superb writer and I want to read more.' co, age 10.

gripping book that has excitement bursting from every page. Isabella is the heart of it all.' Billy, age 11.

f I had to describe it in three words they would be passionate, emotional nd, best of all, extraordinary.' Lalita, age 10.

'I was bubbling with excitement and fresh ideas. We couldn't put it down. A fabulous ending which made you want to read it all over again.' Grace and Ella, age 10.

great read with a gripping plotline. Its interesting and unstoppable aracters seem to jump out of the pages.' Rebecca, age 11.

emotional book, full of excitement and adventure, that describes the gic lives of families during the war. An amazing book.' Mathilda, age

Tears and laughter explode from ev   was so gripping I couldn't ut it down.' Julia, age 11.

never want   so gripping you'll can be torn   uring wars families

TROUBLE ON CABLE STREET

JOAN LINGARD

Catnip

CATNIP BOOKS
Published by Catnip Publishing Ltd
Quality Court, off Chancery Lane
London
WC2A 1HR

This edition first published 2014

1 3 5 7 9 10 8 6 4 2

Text copyright © Joan Lingard, 2014
The moral right of the author has been asserted.

Cover design by Will Steele

A CIP catalogue record for this book is available from the British Library.

ISBN 978-1-84647-1858

Printed by CPI Group (UK) Ltd, Croydon, CR0 4YY

www.catnippublishing.co.uk

For Margaret
and
in remembrance of my father Henry Lingard,
born in Mile End Road
in the East End of London

One

One

Isabella's brothers had a ferocious fight that day. It was to be their last one.

Dusk was creeping in through the alleyways and streets when Isabella emerged from Goldberg's workshop. A stream of dockers passed by, half bent over, heads down, slogging wearily along the pavement on their way home after ten-, eleven-, twelve-hour shifts. At home their women were lighting coal fires. The evenings were drawing in and beginning to cool down. There was a smell of smoke in the air. It was October.

In two days William would leave home to join the war in Spain.

Isabella heard her brothers' voices up ahead as she raced along the street, dodging an unsteady drunk and a couple of women walking arm in arm, while close behind them came another pushing a pram piled high with washing and a small child perched on top. A number of children were still out, turning a skipping rope or sitting on the kerb, barefoot, rolling marbles. Two girls were playing leapfrog. One fell and let out a loud cry. Isabella sped on.

It was Bridie, Isabella's best friend, who had brought the news of the fight to her. Just before seven, Bridie had popped her head round the door of Goldberg's, the tailor's where Isabella worked.

'Issie,' she'd cried, 'they're at it again! Will and Arthur, the two of them in the entry. You'll have to stop them, else they'll kill each other!' Bridie was sweet on William, the younger of Isabella's two brothers.

'Finish that buttonhole first please, Isabella,' Mr Goldberg had said when Bridie came in. 'It should only take you a minute. It's not seven yet.'

It was three minutes to.

'Yes, Mr Goldberg,' said Isabella. Her fingers were aching and her eyes weary. She'd been rubbing them, which only made them worse.

Isabella had been working steadily since seven o'clock that morning, apart from a couple of short breaks. It was no wonder that the tailors' businesses were known as sweatshops. But she had to admit that Mr Goldberg was a fairer employer than some and he even paid a little better. She'd come to work for him when she'd turned fourteen and left school.

She was lucky to have a job, she knew that. Mr

Flynn, Bridie's father, had been out of work for ages and Bridie's mother did odd jobs like taking in washing and scrubbing floors. Bridie herself worked part-time in a grocer's. She'd been employed by Mr Goldberg for a while but her work hadn't been good enough. You had to have nimble fingers and work fast.

Isabella's family fared better than the Flynns. Her dad was a gaffer at the West Dock. Men respected him. He was a local, born and bred in Mile End Road. Even the fact that he had a foreign wife was not held against Jim Blake. His two sons had jobs in the Stores departments at the shipyard and both, like their father, had a reputation for working hard and being reliable.

As soon as Isabella had finished the buttonhole she jumped up and grabbed her coat. The clock was striking seven.

'See you in the morning, Isabella.'

'Yes, Mr Goldberg.'

'Don't be late.'

'No, Mr Goldberg.'

She was never late.

Isabella could hear them clearly now, her two brothers. Born eleven months apart, Will was now seventeen and so was Arthur. They were physically totally unalike, Arthur being fair and blue-eyed like his father, whilst William was dark-haired and brown-eyed like his mother and sister. The brothers were yelling at each other. Not for the first time.

'Fascist pig!'

'Dirty Commie!'

As Isabella turned into the entry she saw William in the act of being felled by a heavy blow from Arthur's fist. Arthur was a boxer. He belonged to a club and took part in competitions. He was tall, topping six feet, and well built, whilst William, though not much shorter, was of slighter build.

'William!' Isabella rushed forward to lift his head and cradle it in her arms. His eyelids flickered open.

'I'm OK,' he muttered.

She looked up at Arthur. 'You could have killed him!'

'Look at my nose!' retorted Arthur. Blood was gushing from it. 'I think it's broken.'

'I don't,' said Isabella, tossing over her handkerchief. William had done well though, to get a blow in. She patted his shoulder. He groaned and she helped him raise his head. He would have a bruiser of an eye come morning. 'Are you all right?'

'I'm fine.' William didn't like a fuss.

'Why do you have to fight, the two of you? What's Dad going to say? He'll be furious.' Isabella felt angry enough with them herself. Why couldn't they just agree to disagree and leave it at that? This business of coming to blows had been happening more and more often recently, and when their father tried to tackle them about their fighting Arthur would walk out.

'Do you know what he's going to do?' demanded Arthur, stabbing his finger at William. 'He's going to Spain. To join the International Brigade and fight for the Republicans! The bloody Commies!'

'Mama's family are for the Republicans,' retorted Isabella. '*They're* not Commies.'

'They're fools.'

'How dare you say that?' Isabella wanted to go over and thump Arthur herself, but she simmered down at the prospect of William going to war. 'You're not, are you, William?'

The thought appalled her. Their father had fought in the Great War between 1914 and 1918. He had joined the navy and served on the *Britannic*, a passenger liner converted to a hospital ship, sister ship of the *Titanic*. They'd struck a German mine off the coast of Greece. Her dad had been lucky to escape with only a mild injury that left him with a stiff shoulder.

Several of their neighbours who had been conscripted into the army had suffered in the trenches in France, losing legs or arms. People couldn't believe that there would be another war in Europe. They feared Adolf Hitler, though. Isabella and Bridie had seen him on the *Pathé Pictorial News* at the pictures, jackbooting up and down, arm extended in a salute and his troops drawn up in ranks, shouting, '*Heil Hitler*!' It was frightening.

'The Nationalists – Franco's men – are killing our cousins!' cried William. 'They're friends of Hitler and Mussolini. They got the Italian air force to bomb Malaga. We don't know if Mama's family is alive or dead. That's why I'm going to Spain.'

They had heard on the wireless that thousands had left the city of Malaga, where their mother's relatives lived, and were fleeing along the coast road. She was desperate for news of her family.

'The Republicans are burning churches,' spat Arthur in return, 'and killing priests. They might have executed Mama's cousin, Father Antonio, for all we know. What do you say to that?'

'Stop it!' cried Isabella, stamping her foot. They had collected a small crowd at the end of the alleyway. 'Now! This very minute! Let's go home.'

She strode ahead, fizzing with anger. Her brothers followed sullenly, keeping their distance from each other.

Bridie was waiting round the corner. When she saw William she rushed forward.

'You're hurt, Will!' she cried.

'That's nothing,' said Arthur. 'Wait till he meets Franco's army full on.'

'Army?' repeated Bridie. 'But we're not at war, are we? The Huns aren't coming, are they?' She sounded scared. The Flynns' next-door neighbour, who had fought in the last war and lost a leg, spent his days leaning against the wall on his crutches with his trouser leg pinned back at the knee.

'No, we are not going to war, Bridie,' said Arthur. 'The Germans are our friends.'

William snorted. 'You're off your head! The Gerries are busy helping Franco kill our family.'

'Stop it!' Isabella stamped her foot again. She wanted to bang her brothers' heads together. 'Come on, Bridie!' She marched off. When her temper was up even her brothers kept back. Bridie had to run to keep up with her. The rubber band that held back Isabella's hair while she was at work had come loose and her long thick black hair flew behind her in the wind.

Two boys suddenly cut across in front of the girls, almost tripping them up. Bridie's eleven-year-old brother was one of them.

'Mickey!' she yelled at him. 'What do you think you're doin'?'

They could see very well what the boys had been up to. They had tied a string to the knockers of two houses next door to each other and rung their bells. Playing 'Knock-Down Ginger', it was called.

The boys disappeared down an alleyway. The inhabitants of the two houses were cursing as they tried to open their doors. Bridie went to their rescue and removed the strings. The two women were red in the face and fuming. 'Them boys! I'd string them up if I got the chance. Did you see them?'

Bridie and Isabella shook their heads and carried on down the street.

'That brother of mine's a right divil, so he is,' Bridie grimaced. Mickey was constantly in trouble of one kind or another. His sister suspected he nicked bars of chocolate and packets of cigarettes and whatever else he could get his hands on, although he always denied it. She worried that he'd end up in more trouble, serious trouble. 'Brothers!' she said.

She had five in all. Sean, the second youngest at fifteen going on sixteen, was the best of the bunch, thought Isabella, and Bridie too. The rest, Kieron, Dominic and Fergal had a reputation for being troublemakers.

Bridie went inside with a promise to come round later and Isabella carried on to her own front door. William and Arthur followed close behind her. They were stony-faced and tight-lipped.

'*Madre mia*!' exclaimed their mother when she saw her two sons. She looked at William's eye. 'What have you been doing?'

Their father came through from the scullery, drying his face and neck on a towel. After work he always stripped to the waist and washed, and had trained his sons to do the same. He looked from one to the other.

'Have you been fighting again? How many times do I have to tell you I will not put up with it?'

'Dad,' broke in Isabella, unable to contain herself, 'Will is going to Spain to join the International Brigade.'

Their mother sank into a chair and covered her face with her hands. She was worried enough about her family caught up in the civil war in Spain, but that her son should go there too! She looked up at William. 'You're not, are you, son?'

'I'm sorry, Mama.' William turned to his father. 'You're on the side of the Republicans, Dad, aren't you?'

'Sides, sides...' moaned their mother. 'My poor country is split in two. How I hate it all!'

'Mama, the Republicans won the election,' said William. 'They should be in power now but General Franco won't accept that, will he, Dad?'

'No, you're right. He will not.'

'Franco and his Nationalists are on the side of the rich and powerful.' William's face grew more and more flushed. 'He wants to grind the poor and the peasants under his heel.'

'And the Republicans want to kill nuns and priests,' snapped his brother.

'The Church wants to control the people,' retorted William.

'That's no reason to kill them.'

'Stop, *stop*!' cried their mother. 'Why do people have

to fight all the time? Why can they not live in peace?'

'Civil war is the worst war of all,' said their father in a low voice. 'Brother against brother. Father against son.'

'But why do *you* have to go, William?' asked his mother. 'This is your country here.'

'Your family is there, Mama. They are part of our family. *My* family. They need help.'

'I know. I know!' She started to weep again and her husband put his arm around her.

'Dad,' William appealed to him, 'if you were younger, would you go?'

His father pursed his lips as he considered. 'I might.'

William turned to his brother. 'You see!'

Arthur shrugged.

Isabella had grown quiet. Will was going to go, she could see that. And even though she didn't want him to, she understood his reasons. He had always been a passionate boy, ready to support causes. What she couldn't understand was why Arthur was so passionately against the Republicans. Did he care so much about the war, one way or another? He had always been less interested, less connected to his Spanish inheritance than either Will or herself.

Their father looked at William. 'When do you go, son?'

'Saturday.'

'Saturday!' cried their mother. 'But that's the day after tomorrow.'

Two

Friday passed in a rush, getting ready for William's departure, what with sorting out his clothes and preparing food for him to eat on the way. Isabella ran to and from the shops fetching provisions for her mother, who was keeping herself busy. She baked William his favourite, a lemon sponge cake, also an apple pie, a batch of almond biscuits and a dozen jam tarts. She fried ten sausages and wrapped them in greaseproof paper. She buttered slices of bread and placed thick slices of cheddar cheese between them. The smell in the house was wonderful.

'Mother,' William protested when he saw the packages of food laid out. 'I won't have room in my rucksack for all that lot.'

'You must eat,' she insisted. 'You have a long journey.'

He argued no further. One way or another he managed to squash it all into his bag.

Isabella and her father normally worked a half-day on Saturdays. But this Saturday was different and both of their employers understood that.

Bridie came along early to say goodbye to William. Tears ran down her face when she came out of the room.

'William is going to be all right,' said Isabella determinedly.

Bridie nodded. Isabella gave her a hug and they clung to each other for a moment.

William's mother also shed tears. Then she said, 'May God go with you, my son, and bring you safely back to me.' She held on to him as if she would never let him go. Their father had to prise him out of her arms.

'William will come back, Maria,' he said gently.

She crossed herself and turned her back so that she would not see them go. She did not want to say goodbye to him in a railway station.

Of Arthur they had seen no sign that morning. He must have risen very early and slipped out. No one had seen him leave.

They didn't talk on the bus. It was crowded and they had to stand. Isabella stared stonily at the back of William's head. She felt as if she were turned to stone. She knew her brother was doing a noble thing, going to fight for a cause he believed in. All their neighbours had applauded him as he walked along the street. They had patted him on the back and said, 'Good on you, Will lad! We have to stand up to these Fascists or we will have them over here next week as soon as you can say Jack Robinson.'

The station was busy. It was a Saturday, of course, although not many workers had the whole day off. Some families looked as if they were going to have a day out in the country or the seaside. They were three days into October, but the weather was still pleasant enough. Some small children carried buckets and spades. Isabella wished they could join them and build castles in the sand.

They recognised the other volunteers straight away. A straggly group of young men in ordinary work clothes with rucksacks on their backs was forming near the stance for the train to Dover. They looked as if they were waiting for someone to tell them what to do. They would cross the channel and then go by train down through France and cross into Spain. They looked cocky, yet uncertain. They reminded Isabella of the men who had come to London from all over Britain to take part in the National Hunger March in 1932, four years earlier. Her dad and Will had joined the march, along with dozens of their neighbours, most of whom were out of work themselves. It had been a huge event but Isabella's dad doubted if it had changed anything.

An older man wearing some kind of military uniform had now joined the group at the barrier. They clustered round him, drawing nearer together, heads bent listening to what he had to say.

'I'd better go,' said William abruptly. 'Don't come!' He shook hands with his father, who then took him by the shoulders and held him tightly against his chest. Isabella saw that her father's eyes were moist but she knew he would not break down into tears.

'Good luck, son,' was all he said. 'We will remember you in our prayers.'

Isabella didn't know her dad said prayers. He didn't go to church, like her mother. It was her turn now to say goodbye to William. She couldn't speak. She just clung to him, her head turned to the side so that he would not see that the tears that were running down her face.

Please God bring him back to us safe and sound, she gabbled inside her head.

William mumbled something but she couldn't make out what it was and then he turned away from them and walked over to join his new comrades. Before they went through the barrier he looked round briefly and waved. They waved back, but he was no longer looking in their direction and soon he was lost in the crowd, gone from their sight.

'Let's go home, love,' said Isabella's father, putting an arm round her shoulder.

They didn't speak until they were almost there.

'He's very brave,' said Isabella, as they turned into their street.

'And so must we be,' said her father.

By the time they pushed open the front door, her mother had calmed down, though her eyes were red and swollen from prolonged weeping.

'William is fine,' her husband reassured her. 'This is something he feels he has to do. *Wants* to do.'

Bridie came in shortly afterwards. 'Has he gone?' she cried.

'Yes,' said Isabella, 'he has gone.'

There was no sign of Arthur all day. He stayed out until after midnight. Isabella, who had been lying awake, heard him come in and exchange a few words with their father before climbing the stairs and going into the room he normally shared with his brother. Their father's voice had sounded sharp. He didn't like his sons coming home so late as he preferred to lock up for the night himself, knowing that everyone was safely in the house.

Isabella stared into the darkness broken only by a glimmer of light coming through the thin curtain from the street lamp outside. From time to time a car swept past, sending a fan of light into the room. She slept in an alcove at the back of the living room, so she heard the low rumble of traffic any time she woke in the night. The noise was comforting. She liked the feeling that the city of London was still alive.

After washing in the scullery, her father was now climbing the stairs, knowing that tonight one of his sons was missing from the house. Where would William be now? In the train rushing through the darkness of the French countryside heading for the Spanish frontier? She imagined him sitting up, along with the other lads, their heads nodding and swaying with the movement of the train.

They had made that journey themselves only two years ago, all five of them, when they had gone to visit their mother's family in Malaga. It had taken two days to cover the length of France and Spain, sitting awkwardly on hard seats, slouched against one another, sleeping for a few minutes then jerking awake, thinking the journey would never end. It was a long way to the south of Spain and the train slowed almost to walking pace at times.

They had emerged, stunned, at the end of the journey into the brilliant summer heat of the city of Malaga, into heavy pungent smells coming from the gutters and the loud cries from people in the streets as they greeted each other. Their mother had smiled. This was her territory and she had not been home for five years. It was the first time her children had set foot in Spain. They hadn't been able to afford to take them before.

Their mother always said she should have made more effort to teach them her language. She should have insisted. Isabella was the best of the three. The boys could say little more than '*Hola!*' and '*Gracias*'. In spite of that, after two weeks in Malaga, when it came to boarding the train for the return journey, they felt that this place was part of them and these people were linked to them. At least Isabella and William did. Not Arthur. Arthur hated the heat that made him sweat from morning to night and brought him out in a rash, as it did their father with his fair skin, though he did not complain. He kept to the shade and mopped his brow with a handkerchief that his wife had scented with cologne.

Arthur hated the eternal hubbub of noise that went on from early morning till late at night and often into the next morning. *Why could people not just speak normally to each other? Why did they have to shout? Was everybody deaf?* Small children ran about until one, two in the morning. Everyone went to bed so late!

And then there was the food, swimming in olive oil! Arthur hated the olive oil and blood sausage and the coarse white bread and sardines and garlic. He hated the smell of garlic on other people's breath. You couldn't avoid their breath, as you were expected to kiss each member of the family every time you met – first one cheek, then the other. Once in the day was not enough. Their mother had seven siblings and each had a

23

number of children so there were a lot of cheeks to be kissed, some of them, in the case of the children, grubby, even sticky. Arthur hated it. His mother teased him, said he was too English. But he liked being English! His mother assured him there was nothing wrong with that. 'I want you to like being what you are.'

Isabella and William had loved everything Arthur hated. She smiled into the darkness, remembering the trip as if it were yesterday. They had promised to save up and return to Spain. And now William was on his way there.

Three

Arthur went out early next morning. Isabella saw him leaving. He was neatly dressed, as usual on weekends, with a collar and tie and his hair brushed back. He would not be going to church. Their mother thought he might have a sweetheart. But Arthur was secretive, he never gave anything away.

'Where are you going?' Isabella had asked.

'Out,' was all he had said and went, closing the street door behind him.

She should have known better than to expect a reply.

Their father was in the scullery, shaving in front of the mirror, concentrating intently, drawing the razor carefully up over his cheek towards his ear, leaving a clear strip behind. She stood watching him.

'Where's Arthur gone?' she asked.

Her father shrugged. He made a point of not asking his sons where they were going after they passed their fourteenth birthday, but he still asked his daughter. He fussed more over her, didn't like her to come back a minute or two later at night than she had promised.

'Has Mama gone to church?' she asked.

'Yes. She was going to see if you'd go with her but you were fast asleep.'

Isabella had been dreaming of William, sitting on a train that never seemed to arrive. The journey had gone on and on, passing through stations, not stopping. She remembered the dream vividly. She could hear the chugging of the wheels and see the spiral of smoke coming from the engine, drifting backwards, leaving a trace behind it after the train itself had gone.

'I wonder where William is now. Do you think he will have got there yet?'

Her dad shrugged. Neither of them knew where 'there' was.

'I wish he hadn't gone,' she said unnecessarily.

'Well he has. And we have to live with it.'

Her dad sluiced his face under the cold tap, removing the last traces of soap, then he wiped the razor clean and put it back into its sheath.

'I'm going to meet your mother at the church and take her to Kew Gardens for the day. You know how she loves flowers. There might still be some blooming. It's a long winter for her here. I'd have liked to take her back to Malaga for a week or two this autumn. But it's out of

26

the question now, of course.' He pulled on a clean white shirt and fixed a starched collar on to it. 'Not that we're without troubles ourselves.'

'Do you think we'll go to war, Dad? With Germany?' asked Isabella anxiously. 'Everybody's talking about it.'

'Depends if the German people let Hitler get away with it. He's persecuting the Jews.' Her dad shook his head.

Some of them, like Mr Goldberg, who had managed to escape, were living amongst them in London now.

Her father buttoned up his shirt and was now putting on his tie, Paisley patterned in shades of dark blue and red, a birthday present from his wife. He was particular about his appearance, especially on non-working days, and had encouraged his sons to follow in his ways. He had been more successful as regards dress with Arthur than William.

'There could be trouble at Whitechapel today, Isabella,' he said, as he shrugged his shoulders into his jacket.

Isabella had heard some rumours about a protest march. 'Whitechapel? Why there?'

'Oswald Mosley – you know, the Fascist leader? – well, he's organising a march through the East End with his followers, the Blackshirts, and the police have been stupid enough to give them permission. There is going to be a huge protest against them, by all accounts. People are coming in from all over the country. Communists. Socialists. Trade Unionists.' Jim Blake regarded himself in the mirror, tweaked his tie a little straighter.

'Dad, I thought you might have been against Mosley and the Blackshirts yourself?'

'I am. But I need to take your mother out, away from here. She's had enough, what with worrying about her family in Spain, and now William going. Besides, I think it may turn nasty. There'll be troublemakers in amongst them. Bound to be. So stay away from Whitechapel, Isabella, all right?' He took a last look at himself in the mirror, said, 'We won't be late back,' and then he was off.

Isabella made herself a mug of tea and a piece of toast. She had just finished eating when there came a tap on the door and then it opened.

'Can I come in?' asked Bridie.

'Course. Want a cup of tea?'

'No, ta. Just had one.' Bridie seemed excited. 'Everybody's making for Whitechapel.'

'Dad said to stay away.'

Bridie made a face. 'Oh, what harm can it do, just to go and see? I'd like to get a look at that man. What's his name again?'

'Oswald Mosley.'

He was regarded as an ogre in most parts of the East End, though not all. Bridie had heard that he and his followers planned to round up all the Jews and Irish and shoot them. Isabella was scornful of that. There were always stories going round.

'The boys have gone,' said Bridie. 'They've been helping to build a blockade with rocks and boulders, anything they can get their hands on. Down towards the river.'

'Sean too?'

Bridie nodded. 'C'mon, Issie!!'

'All right, let's go,' said Isabella, getting up. She hadn't taken much persuading. She was as curious as Bridie to see what was going on.

As they opened the door a posse of police on horseback went clopping past. People were milling about in the streets. Lots of people. Isabella thought it was unlikely Mr Goldberg would be out today. When there was any trouble afoot he would draw his curtains and retreat with his wife and children to the back of the house.

At every intersection more people joined the throng. It was amazing how fast everything was happening. Within minutes they found themselves being borne along by the crowd as if by a strong running river, which had swollen so much that no vehicle or policeman on horseback could pass in the road, nor could anybody falter or try to turn back. They had no choice but to go with the flow or be trampled on. Bridie clutched Isabella's hand. They mustn't let go of each other or lose their balance.

'They've cancelled the march,' a man up ahead yelled, his voice so clear that he must have been using a loud hailer.

'No!' roared the crowd, fired up by now.

'Yes!' came back the reply. 'They've been rerouted.'

The crowd pushed on.

Bridie took Isabella's arm. They turned down one side street and then another, zigzagging their way southwards towards the river. That was where everyone seemed to be going.

As they reached Cable Street the crowd swelled, if that was possible, to a size even greater than before. The mood was beginning to change. It was becoming nasty. Some people looked as if they would like to escape but could not. The stream of people was pulling them all southwards and the nearer they drew to the river the stronger the force became.

'Hang on, Bridie,' cried Isabella.

And then, all of a sudden, they came to a complete standstill. The girls struggled to keep their on feet now as people pressed against their backs, trying to shove them forward. They had come to see Mosley and his men and were not going to give up. Glancing round, Isabella saw that they were close to the wall of a house.

'Come on,' she shouted and tugged Bridie's hand.

They managed to scramble up on to a high windowsill,

from where they could see over the heads of the excited crowd.

'Police!' yelled the voice on the loud hailer up ahead. 'They've got the horses out. Move back! *Move back*!'

How could anyone move anywhere, back, forward or sideways? The crowd was solid. The girls clung to each other. People began to elbow and shove. Panic was beginning to set in. A woman and a small child toppled over and were instantly lost from sight amongst the marchers' legs. They could be trampled to death.

Isabella screamed. 'Help them up!' she cried, pointing.

Two strong-shouldered men, with a good deal of shoving, pushing and swearing, made a hole in the crowd.

'Keep back, would you!' yelled one of them. 'Somebody's hurt.'

The men finally succeeded in lifting up the woman and her child – a boy of no more than three or four years – from the pavement. The mother's eyes were wide with terror and her son's head was bleeding at the temple. He was screaming. She was weeping.

'Shouldn't have brought a child like that on the march,' said a woman, turning to Isabella.

Isabella didn't reply. The woman looked argumentative. She had a hard face, though she was probably right.

The two men were still trying to hold back the crowd

31

and clear a space where the woman and her child could stand up. Some people were reluctant to give way.

'Let them through, for God's sake!' shouted a tall man over the heads of the crowd. 'They need help.'

From somewhere up ahead, they could hear shouts and screams at the sound of horses' hooves. A number of marchers were doing their best to turn back and worm their way through the sea of bodies; others were determined to push on, to see what was going on and not let anyone get in their way. The mood was growing angrier now. People wanted to see, shout at, jeer at, throw a brick at Oswald Mosley – friend of Adolf Hitler and Mussolini! He had no right to come on to their territory with his gang. Why did the police allow them to come? Whose side were they on? The crowd pushed even harder. It would not be long before someone else got hurt. Sure enough, there, right in front of them, two women went down sprawling on their stomachs and another fell on top of them. Children were crying.

'Hang on, Bridie!' shouted Isabella. They weren't safe where they were. She had noticed a slightly recessed doorway a few steps back. They slid down from their perches and, keeping a firm grip of Bridie's hand, Isabella dragged her inch by inch into the space. They leaned against the door, glad to have the chance to catch their breath. Bridie was gasping. She had asthma, so Isabella's father thought, but Bridie's mother wouldn't take her to the doctor's even when Mr Blake had offered to pay. She'd said it was only a cough. Didn't half the folk along the street not have coughs? It was the smog. Bridie's dad had bad lungs too.

The girls were in the narrow doorway of a two-storey terraced house. Its windows had been boarded up on both levels. They'd seen a few blanked out like that when they were coming down the road. There could be a Jewish family lying low behind the door, in the dark, listening to the roar of the crowd, scarcely daring to breathe. The Blackshirts were no friends of the Jews.

By standing on her toes Isabella could see the police on horseback now, or part of them, enough to see a truncheon coming up and then being brought down hard. On a marcher's head, no doubt. Up went another truncheon. She gasped. They had to get away from there.

'Hang on to me, Bridie,' she said, 'and don't let go!'

Isabella led the way. It was a struggle trying to carve out a passage through such a solid mass of bodies. They were kicked in the shins and the backs of their legs, but finally they saw light ahead and made it into the clear air. They stopped to catch their breath.

'I thought we was done for there, Issie,' said Bridie.

So did Isabella. She'd never been trapped in a crowd like that before. 'Come on, Bridie!' she said. 'We're going home!'

Bridie's mother, Mrs Flynn, was standing at her door in her apron, her hair flattened close to her head and ridged with steel curlers, just as she was to be seen every day of the week, including Sunday. Once, when Isabella was small, maybe four or five years old, she'd asked Mrs Flynn if she took the curlers out at night so that she'd look nice for Mr Flynn coming home from the pub and had been told not to be so cheeky.

'What's goin' on?' asked Mrs Flynn.

'A riot,' said Isabella.

'Thought it'd come to that,' said Mrs Flynn. 'I told those boys not to go, but do you think they ever listen to me? Their dad warned them there'd be trouble.'

Mr Flynn had been right of course. As had Isabella's father.

Isabella took Bridie along to her house. There was nobody at home. She made a pot of tea and gave Bridie a large mugful and a jam sandwich.

As she ate and drank the colour gradually came back into Bridie's face and her breathing settled. 'That was frightening,' she said.

Isabella nodded.

There came a thump on the door and then it burst open to admit Bridie's brother, Sean.

'Our Kieron's been arrested,' he cried. 'The police dragged him off and threw him into the back of one of their vans. They kicked him first and then they threw him in like a sack of spuds!'

Bridie burst into tears.

Isabella saw that Sean had blood on his face too. Suddenly, he folded up and collapsed on to the sofa. The girls went to him.

'Are you all right, Sean?' asked Bridie tearfully.

'It's nothing,' he groaned, adding, 'there's a lad outside called Robbie. He's in a bad way.'

'Who's Robbie?' asked Isabella. But she didn't wait for an answer. She went out to look and found, sitting on the pavement, his head lolling against the wall, a boy close to collapse. He too was bleeding. 'Hold on to me,' she told him. 'Let's get you inside.'

The boy staggered in on her arm and she helped him into the alcove and let him lie down on her bed.

'I'll go and heat some water, Bridie,' she said. 'We need to clean them up.'

She had no time to do it before the door opened again. Her parents had returned home.

'We were lucky it didn't rain –' Her mother was in the middle of speaking when she stopped abruptly, clapped her hand over her mouth and cried, '*Madre mia*! Sean, what have you been doing?'

Jim Blake went over to the sofa to see for himself. He frowned. 'You've got a bad wound there, lad. What happened?'

'It was the police,' said Isabella.

'They've taken our Kieron away,' sobbed Bridie.

'Is this true?'

'They've arrested him,' said Sean dully.

'You don't look that great yourself,' said Isabella's father. 'I think we might need to find a doctor or take you along to hospital.'

'No, not a hospital!' The thought obviously alarmed Sean. 'The police . . .' His voice trailed off.

'The other boy's worse,' said Isabella. 'I put him on my bed.'

Her dad went to look at him, as did her mother, who gasped when she saw his wounds.

'He came in with Sean,' said Isabella.

'What's his name? Do you know?'

'Robbie, that's all.'

'Robbie,' repeated her father, 'can you hear me?'

The boy nodded, his head rolling to the side.

'We met at the march,' explained Sean.

'I warned you young people not to go. Isabella, did you go too?' asked her father.

'We turned back when we saw there was trouble up ahead.'

'There was no march in the end,' muttered Sean. 'Not in Cable Street. The police rerouted it further along the Embankment to avoid the crowd.'

'Jim,' said his wife, 'we mustn't wait. We need a doctor.

This boy is badly wounded. Look at the blood!' She held up her handkerchief.

'I could go and see if Doctor Gebler would come out,' offered Isabella.

'Go then!' said her father.

'Will I come?' Bridie got up.

'No, I'll be quicker alone.'

Isabella, once outside, took to her heels and raced down the road. There were people gathered in groups all the way along, talking over the events of the day. One or two called to her, but she didn't stop. She turned down the street where they had been earlier in the middle of the crush of people. It was quieter now. The doctor's house was boarded up. She rapped on the door with her knuckles and spoke to him through the letter box.

'Doctor Gebler, it's me, Isabella, Jim Blake's daughter.'

She waited. A moment later a bolt was drawn back and she saw the doctor's face peering at her in the dim light.

'Is that you, Isabella?'

'Yes, Doctor. Can you come, please! Our neighbour's son Sean has been wounded. And another young lad who was on the march. They were beaten up by the police.'

'One minute. I will fetch my bag.'

Dr Gebler walked with a limp. It was said that he

had suffered at the hands of the Nazis before managing to escape from Vienna. He never spoke of it, nor of his relatives there. Isabella slowed her pace to keep abreast of him.

When they reached the house and Dr Gebler saw his two patients he frowned and pursed his lips. He wasted no time or words. 'Hot water, if you please, madam. Boiled.'

Isabella's mother had some ready. They stood back to give the doctor space in which to work.

'They should be in hospital,' he said, removing his jacket and rolling up his shirtsleeves. 'Both of them.'

'No!' cried Sean.

Dr Gebler didn't argue. He knew as well as they did that the police might do a tour of the hospitals looking for troublemakers. He cleaned the boys' wounds and covered them with gauze and sticking plaster. When they cried out in pain Isabella bunched her hands into fists to control her anger. Bridie put her back to the room to hide her tears.

When Dr Gebler had finished and gone out to the scullery to wash his hands the living-room door opened.

'Arthur!' exclaimed his mother. 'Where have you been?'

He didn't answer. He stood staring at the two boys with their bandaged heads. 'Don't tell me you went on the protest march, Sean!' he said.

'What if he did?' demanded Isabella.

'Fool!'

'Don't speak to Sean like that!' said their father sharply.

But Arthur had no time for any of the Flynn boys. He always said they didn't know how to stay out of trouble, which was largely true. They had quick tempers, but they could be charming too.

Arthur looked at his father. 'You said yourself it would be a good idea to stay away. I heard there were thousands of them at the march. Commies, hooligans, just out to cause trouble. They're still out there, all over the place, causing mayhem.'

'I shall leave you now,' said Dr Gebler. 'You know what to do if their temperatures rise in the night, Mrs Blake? Sponge them down with cold cloths and give them plenty of fluid. If the fever gets very bad come for me.'

'We will manage, Doctor. I have nursed my younger sisters. And Isabella will help me.'

Isabella nodded.

'Perhaps I –' Bridie began, but Isabella's mother interrupted her.

'Two pairs of hands will do, my dear. Too many – what do you say – spoil broth?'

At least she had raised a smile, if only fleetingly.

'What do we owe you, Doctor?' asked Jim Blake

'Nothing, Mr Blake. Absolutely not!' Dr Gebler said his goodbyes and left them.

'And where have you spent the day, Arthur?' asked his father in a low voice.

Arthur shrugged. 'Around. Not in Cable Street anyway.' He turned away as he said it, Isabella noticed, as if he had something to hide. So where had he been? Surely not . . . Isabella let that thought slide. Arthur had a couple of friends she disliked, arrogant boys, a year or two older than him.

The door opened again and Mrs Flynn put her head round it. 'Have any of youse seen my Sean?' When she saw the state he was in she went into hysterics. Bridie calmed her down and took her home. They were all agreed that Sean would be better left in the care of Maria Blake, who was widely reputed in the street to have healing hands.

Arthur gestured towards Robbie. 'Where's he from?'

'Glasgow, I think,' muttered Sean, wincing as he spoke.

Arthur fixed his stare on Robbie. 'So you came all the way down from Glasgow, just to cause trouble?'

'That's enough, Arthur,' said his father. 'I will not have you insult a guest in our house.'

'Some guest,' retorted Arthur and turning on his heel he left the house again, slamming the door behind him.

'What's happening?' wailed his mother. 'Suddenly everyone is fighting!'

Four

Neither Isabella nor her mother had any sleep that night. They put Sean on the sofa and laid a palliasse on the floor for Robbie. Both boys were feverish much of the time and at one point Robbie's temperature soared so high they were tempted to call the doctor.

'Do you think we should, Mama?' asked Isabella anxiously. 'He is very hot.'

He was moaning, half-awake, half-unconscious. He didn't seem to know where he was. His head lolled from side to side. 'Where . . . ?' he began, then his voice trailed away.

'You're in London,' Isabella told him, as she applied cold compresses to his forehead.

'London?' he repeated, as if it might be the moon.

'You are with *amigos*,' said Isabella's mother.

'Friends,' Isabella translated for him.

But Robbie was beyond understanding anything in any language.

'His poor mother will be wondering what has happened to him,' said Maria Blake. 'Who would be a mother!' This was always her cry whenever her boys got into trouble.

Sean had finally drifted off not long after midnight and seemed a little less restless, though at intervals he talked in his sleep and at one point cried out, 'No! No!' and flailed his arms about.

They sat in armchairs on either side of the fire, Isabella and her mother. Isabella got up from time to time to put on another lump of coal. Arthur came home in the early hours, not saying a word. They dozed a bit. By the time light was beginning to filter through the curtains the invalids were fast asleep and their breathing had changed, becoming steadier and more rhythmic.

'That is good sign,' said Isabella's mother. 'We leave them now and go to the kitchen for a cup of tea.'

Isabella put the kettle on to boil. She poured the tea and had just taken a sip when there was a knock on the front door, announcing the arrival of Dr Gebler. He had come to check up on the invalids. He took off his bowler hat and passed it to Isabella, who laid it on the sideboard.

'How good of you to come, Doctor!' exclaimed her mother.

He was pleased to see that the boys were sleeping, but frowned when he tried Robbie's pulse and slid a thermometer under his tongue. 'You will need to keep an eye on him, Mrs Blake.'

'Oh, we will. Do not worry for that! Can we offer you cup of tea, Doctor, freshly made?'

But Dr Gebler would not stop. He had several more patients to attend to before he went home to bed. He shook his head. 'What brutality I have seen! I would not have thought it of the British police.'

'I think everything got out of hand,' said Jim Blake, coming down the stairs to join them. 'I don't think they expected such big numbers. Not that I excuse them. Certainly not!'

'I will wish you good day then, now,' said Dr Gebler, giving them a small bow before replacing his bowler hat. 'If you need me do not hesitate to call.'

'Thank you, Doctor,' said Jim Blake.

'He looked terrible,' said Isabella's mother after the doctor had gone. 'He hasn't been to bed. And he is not young.'

'You don't look so good yourself, my love,' said her husband. 'I think you could do with some rest.'

But how could she go to bed and leave Sean and Robbie alone? They both needed attention and the workers in the house must soon leave.

'Why doesn't Sean's mother come and take him home?' demanded Arthur when he came downstairs. 'They only live along the road. He shouldn't have to stay here.' He didn't want any breakfast. He would get something to eat at a workmen's café near the docks. He didn't ask after the invalids' health, giving them a scant look before leaving.

Isabella wanted to shout after him, 'Don't you care about anyone but yourself?' But she had the feeling he was not easy with himself. He would not look her in the eye these days.

On her way to work Isabella pushed open the Flynns' door and called out, 'It's me, Isabella.'

Mrs Flynn was still in her nightdress, smoking the usual cigarette.

Bridie came through from the scullery. 'How's Sean?' she asked straight away.

'A bit better. We had Dr Gebler in again.'

'That's real good of your mother taking him in like that,' said Mrs Flynn. 'I was just saying to Paddy she'd make a grand nurse, so she would.'

'Do you not think we should bring him home now, Mam?' asked Bridie. She turned to Isabella. 'Your mum will be tired.'

Isabella nodded. 'She is a bit.'

'I'll get Dominic up and we'll go and fetch him.'

'If Sean's comfy . . .' started Mrs Flynn.

'Mam, Mrs Blake must be tired out,' insisted Bridie.

'I must be going,' said Isabella. 'Else I'll be late for work.' She didn't know how she would get through

44

the day. Twelve hours of sewing seams, or even worse, buttonholes, except for two ten-minute breaks and a half hour for lunch. Her eyes were aching even before she started that morning.

Mr Goldberg, though, for once, was sympathetic. 'You may leave early if you wish, Isabella.' He was aware how much the trouble of the previous day had affected everyone. There was an uneasy quiet around the streets of the East End.

Isabella knew she would lose money by finishing early, but that could not be helped. Mr Goldberg would never pay for work not done, no matter the circumstances. After all, he too had to make a living.

She took a different route home. She wanted to spend just a little more time in the fresh air. Some of the streets still showed signs of yesterday's battle. Dropped litter. Somebody's trampled hat. Broken windows boarded up. On a gable-end wall there was graffiti in slashes of yellow paint.

PERISH THE JEWS

卐

She thought of Arthur and shivered. Surely he wouldn't do a thing like that? No, of course he wouldn't. Splashing paint around would not be his style. What was? Attending meetings of the BUF? The British Union of Fascists. Their father would have a fit if he thought any of his children were going near them.

She passed a rooming house with a notice in the window which read, *No Jews. No Blacks. No Irish.* She'd seen it before and not thought much about it. Bridie's brother Kieron had chucked a stone through the window of that house once when they were all a few years younger. They'd taken to their heels and run like the clappers.

When she arrived home she found the house quiet. Her mother was asleep in her bedroom, as was Robbie, upstairs in William's bed. When she looked in and saw his head on the pillow she thought for one fleeting moment that it was William himself who lay there and her heart leapt. Then she realised that of course it could not be William. He would have arrived in Spain by now. And this boy had red hair.

There was no sign of Sean.

She lay down on her bed, fully dressed, and slept a little, but when she dozed off she dreamed she was running along a station platform beside a moving train that would not stop even though she shouted at the top of her voice and waved her arms about. When she wakened she found her throat was sore. She got up and checked William's room. Robbie was still asleep so she and her mother decided to leave him be.

Jim Blake returned from work with a bundle of the

day's newspapers under his arm. He bought papers every day and read them from cover to cover. He liked to keep abreast of what was going on in the world, especially Spain of course. There were a number of pictures of Mosley in his military uniform. In one he had his right arm raised in a Nazi salute.

'He seems to think he's Mussolini in that outfit,' said Isabella's dad. He shook his head in disgust, folded the paper and chucked it to one side. 'Let's eat! Are you going to your class this evening, Isabella?'

Isabella nodded. In spite of being tired she would go. She hated to miss a class. She was training to be a stenographer in the hope of getting a job in an office some day. She didn't intend to spend the rest of her life sewing buttonholes.

Arthur came in and went into the scullery to wash before eating. He joined them at the table.

'How was work today, Arthur?' asked his father.

'All right.' Arthur shrugged. He hated his job in the shipyard Stores. It was boring him to death, he said. He was lucky not to be a docker, his father reminded him whenever he complained, loading and unloading all day long. That was tougher. His father had started out that way before becoming a supervisor. Most of the dockers had no job security either. They just had to queue up each morning hoping to be taken on for the day.

'Shall I take some soup up to Robbie?' asked Isabella.

'Is he still here?' asked Arthur, irritably. 'Why doesn't he go home?'

'To Glasgow?' put in Isabella. 'It's a long way.'

'He is not in a good state to move,' said her mother decisively.

'So is he in my room?' asked Arthur.

'He is in William's bed,' said his mother. 'That is what William would have wanted.'

Arthur looked as if he was about to reply and then thought better of it. He lifted a hunk of bread and started to eat the plate of stewed chorizo sausage his mother had placed in front of him. The mention of William had quietened them.

Robbie's fever grew worse during the night and eventually they had to seek help again. Arthur's father woke him and told him to go and rouse Dr Gebler. Arthur grumbled but he pulled on his clothes and went. He knew when not to argue with his father. Isabella put the kettle on for a cup of tea. Her mother, who had been nursing Robbie most of the evening into the night, looked exhausted.

'Go to bed, Mama.'

'How can I?' She pressed a cold compress against Robbie's forehead.

Isabella didn't argue. She looked at the boy's face. He

had freckles sprinkled across his nose and a scar running down the side of his left cheek. She sighed. He was a stranger to them, yet surely there must be somebody, somewhere, missing him, wondering where he was.

Arthur returned within a few minutes to announce that the doctor was either asleep, not at home, or not answering. 'There were no lights in the house.'

'Did you knock loudly?' asked Isabella.

'Loudly enough.'

'What does that mean?'

'Perhaps he's had enough of people knocking him up in the night to come and treat hooligans.'

'Robbie is no hooligan,' retorted Isabella.

'How do you know what he is?'

'He is ill, Arthur.'

'So what can we do about it?'

'I don't know.' Their father pursed his lips. 'Perhaps we should call an ambulance.'

'If they take him to hospital they'll know he was on the march,' said Isabella.

'Better that than being dead. You could try Dr Gordon, Arthur,' said his father.

Arthur sighed. 'OK, I'll take the bike and go and see if Dr Gordon is around.'

Dr Gordon lived further away but he had a car, unlike Dr Gebler, who went everywhere on foot.

'You are a good boy, Arthur,' said his mother fondly.

He was on the whole, thought Isabella. She had seen him carrying old Mrs Craddock's shopping along the street only a couple of days ago. She hadn't tried to catch them up for she knew he would prefer not to be seen. He was good mannered, as was William. Their father had dinned that into them all from when they were young. Their mother said it was their father's manners that had attracted her to him in the beginning. She had come to London expecting all men to be the same as he was. She had been disappointed, of course.

'Mind how you go, Arthur,' warned his father. 'Those brakes aren't working. It's time you did something about them.'

'William was supposed to sort it.'

'Well he can't now, can he?'

Isabella went with Arthur out to the shed in the back yard to collect the bike. The handlebars were slightly twisted. He straightened them. The front wheel didn't look too good either.

'Do be careful,' said Isabella.

'You're getting as bad as Mother!'

She watched him as he swerved out from the kerb on the rickety bike. The trams and buses had stopped running. There wasn't much traffic on the road at this time of night, unlike in the daytime when the street buzzed with vehicles. Isabella stood there for a moment.

The pavement, damp from a quick shower of rain, glinted under the lamplight. She listened to the faint hum of traffic. London never slept. The Flynns' ginger cat slunk past. A drunk reeled out of a doorway, muttering something, shaking his fist at the sky. Isabella went back inside.

Dr Gordon arrived in his little Morris Minor before Arthur was back.

'That is good for you to come out at this hour, Doctor,' said their mother.

'It is my job, dear lady. So you have a sick man in the house?'

Their father took him straight away up the stairs while Isabella and her mother waited below. The clock on the mantelpiece struck two.

'You won't get much sleep again tonight, Isabella,' said her mother.

'Nor will you, Mama.'

'But you have to go to work. I can doze during the day. Mr Goldberg would not like it if you did that.'

'No, he would not!'

Arthur returned just as the doctor and their father were coming down the stairs.

'He has a very high fever, I'm afraid,' said Dr Gordon. 'Dangerously high. I'll have to call an ambulance. And I don't like the look of the wound on his head. It's gone septic.'

'The poor boy,' cried their mother.

'Do you know anything about him?'

They shook their heads.

'We think he might be Scottish,' said Isabella. 'From Glasgow, possibly.'

'And his name?'

'Robbie.'

'You don't know his surname?'

'No.'

'He seems to have no identification on him. I presume he was a casualty of the march?'

'It would appear so,' said Jim Blake.

'Ah well, there are a few around this morning. But I'll need to get along to the hospital now. They should send an ambulance fairly soon. Depends how busy they are.'

Dr Gordon, like Dr Gebler, refused payment. He bade them goodnight.

Isabella went back upstairs with her mother. The heat coming from the invalid made the bedroom feel as if it was on fire.

'Get some cold water, Isabella,' instructed her mother.

Isabella brought a basin and together she and her mother applied wet cloths to Robbie's forehead. His eyes were closed, his breathing shallow.

It took half an hour for the ambulance to come. The women left the bedroom to give the ambulance men more space to settle the patient on the stretcher. Slowly they manipulated the stretcher down the narrow staircase, taking care not to give the patient a jolt.

'You're going to be all right, Robbie,' Isabella said softly, bending over him before they took him out. 'They'll take good care of you at the hospital.'

'Anyone accompanying him?' asked one of the men.

'I'll go,' said Jim Blake immediately, reaching for his jacket.

'You don't have to, Dad,' said Arthur. 'He's nothing to us.'

'Arthur!' cried Isabella.

'Well, it's true! He's a stranger, isn't he?'

Jim Blake made no comment but he looked displeased. He followed the men out.

'Your father would not let the poor lad go alone, Arthur, without mother or father,' said his mother.

'I just thought we'd done enough for him,' said Arthur and went upstairs to get a couple of hours' sleep.

His mother shook her head. 'That boy, he's worrying me.'

'Go to bed, Mama,' said Isabella. 'You look done in.'

Her mother didn't argue this time.

Isabella lay down on the sofa and dozed until her dad came back. He had nothing new to tell them other than that Robbie had been admitted.

'I'll call in at the hospital on my way back from work and see how he's doing. And now let's see if we can get a little sleep.'

Isabella was home before her father. She had managed to get through the day even though she couldn't stop yawning. She'd told Mr Goldberg about Robbie, so he had not scolded her when she'd had to redo two buttonholes. How she hated buttonholes! But she would not sew them forever. Her teacher at the evening class said her typing skills were excellent and she was making good progress at shorthand. Soon she would be able to sit the exam. That thought kept her going.

She was working at her shorthand when her father came in from work. She looked up.

'Did you go to the hospital?'

He nodded and sat down. He sighed.

Isabella looked at him anxiously. 'Is Robbie in a bad way?'

'He died this afternoon, I'm afraid. They couldn't save him.'

Five

Isabella was so shocked she couldn't speak for a moment and then she cried out, 'He can't be dead!'

'I'm afraid he is, love. I thought he looked as if he was sinking when they took him away.' Her father shook his head. 'What a waste!'

Isabella and her mother shed tears for Robbie, a boy whom they'd known but briefly.

'His poor mother!' said Maria, crossing herself.

'And we don't know where she lives,' cried Isabella.

'That's the problem,' said her dad. 'We don't know his address or his surname. We only knew him as Robbie.'

'Sean might know a bit more. I'll go and ask him.' Isabella set off and met Bridie coming out of her door.

'I was just coming along to ask you about Robbie.'

'He's dead,' said Isabella flatly. She felt blunted inside. Yesterday, this boy Robbie had been alive. He'd sat propped up against the pillows for a while and spoken to them. He'd told them he was sorry for all the bother he was giving them.

'Dead,' repeated Bridie. '*No!*'

'Yes, it's dreadful,' said Isabella. 'How's Sean?'

'A lot better. I'll fetch him.' Bridie came back with her brother.

'That's terrible so it is,' Sean said straight away, 'about Robbie. D'you know, I didn't think he was hurt that bad. I thought he'd be over it in a day or two.'

'Sean,' said Isabella, 'did he say where he was from?'

'Glasgow, wasn't it? There were a number of them in a bunch and one of them was carrying a Trade Union flag. I'm pretty sure it had Glasgow printed on it.' He shook his head. 'Don't suppose any of them are around now. They'll have gone home.'

'How can we find out where he lived?'

'It's a big city, is it not, Glasgow?'

'I think so. Not as big as London but still . . . he didn't tell you his second name, I suppose?'

'There wasn't much chat, with everything going on.'

'No, there wouldn't be.' Isabella bit her lip.

'I just knew he was called Robbie because one of his mates shouted at him to get back.'

'But he didn't?' said Bridie.

'He didn't have a chance. He got kicked on the head by a horse's hoof.'

There seemed nothing more to be said. An unknown

boy had crossed their lives for a mere twenty-four hours and now was gone. They'd never forget him, though.

Later that evening, the local bobby called at the Blakes' house asking about Robbie.

'We need to let his next of kin know,' said PC MacDade.

'I'm afraid we can't help you there,' said Jim Blake. 'We hardly knew the lad. Only that he was called Robbie and came from Glasgow. He had nothing on him, I take it?'

The constable shook his head. 'He'd only a couple of bob and a tram ticket in his trouser pocket. Two shillings wouldn't have got him far. Certainly not back to Glasgow.'

'I suppose –' Isabella hesitated for a moment – 'you couldn't, well, phone the police in Glasgow?' She knew, as soon as she'd said it, that it was a daft suggestion. How could the police track down a missing boy of maybe sixteen or seventeen years with reddish hair called Robbie? Then she thought, *Well, why not?* His mother or father might have gone to the police themselves to report him missing.

'We'll send them up a description,' said PC MacDade. 'Just in case someone's been looking for him. Depends on his family, what they're like. And if he had one.'

That silenced Isabella. She could imagine Robbie might well have been homeless. There had been something about him that made you think that. He hadn't had much flesh on his bones, as her own mother had commented, and his clothes looked shabby and uncared for.

'I suppose he was out on that protest in Cable Street?' said the constable.

Isabella looked at her dad, hoping he wouldn't bring Sean into it and he didn't.

'We presume so,' her father said, looking the constable levelly in the eye.

'How did he come to your house then, him being a stranger to you?'

'A neighbour found him in the street.'

'Ah well,' sighed the constable, 'I thought they shouldn't have let that Mosley fellow have his rally in the first place. Stirs up nothing but trouble, he does. Don't quote me on that, though,' he added hastily. 'Some people think he's all right.'

'Of course not,' said Jim Blake.

PC MacDade put on his helmet and moved towards the door.

'Constable,' said Isabella quickly, 'where is he to be buried? Robbie?'

'Oh, we can't do nothing about a burial, not unless we find his next of kin.'

'You will try then? To find them? It would be terrible . . .' Her voice trailed away. It would be terrible if Robbie were to be left lying in the morgue.

'We'll do what we can. But I wouldn't hold out your

58

hopes. Lots of homeless young men hanging about in the city. Too many.' He sighed. 'Aye, it's hard times right enough.'

'You'll let us know if you did find anything?'

'I'll make a point of it. Don't worry. You seem very concerned about this unfortunate young lad?'

Isabella didn't give him an answer and he didn't wait for one. He bade them goodnight.

Isabella was thinking of William. What if he were to be found dead, stripped of his identity, and they were not informed? They would never then know what had happened to him. They had heard on the wireless of dead Republican supporters being thrown into mass graves. One report said that the poet Federico Garcia Lorca had been executed by a fascist firing squad and his body buried somewhere outside Granada. Isabella's mother loved his poetry. She quoted a couple of lines from one of his poems now.

'*Tell the moon to come out*

For I do not want to see the blood of Ignacio on the sand . . .'

Isabella shivered at the idea of William's blood lying on the sand.

The next day, she considered what they might do to try to track down Robbie's identity. She talked to Sean about it in the evening.

'I don't think the police are going to bother their heads

about it,' he said. 'Got other things to do. Like locking up lads like our Kieron.'

Kieron had been held for a night in the cells for disturbance of the peace and released in the morning with a caution. Next time it would be court and a fine, which he wouldn't be able to pay.

'You're probably right,' agreed Isabella. 'Robbie's nothing to them.' But surely he must be something to somebody? Or perhaps not. It was a terrible thought.

'Coming out?' asked Sean.

Isabella nodded.

They fell into step beside each other and drifted down the street. When the smell of the chip shop reached them Sean said, 'Fancy some hot peas in vinegar?' They were Sean's favourite, even more than chips.

'Wouldn't mind.'

There was a queue. Sean's mother was behind the counter scooping chips into pokes of paper. She looked hot and her hair was sticking to her scalp. She was working four nights a week in the shop these days. Mrs Flynn was usually allowed to bring leftovers home, which her family would then have for breakfast. Bridie complained that the house smelled of fish and chips at night after her mum came home. Isabella's mother was glad not to have to do work like that. She considered herself lucky to have a husband like Jim Blake, who earned a decent living wage.

'I don't need you to tell me what you're wantin', Sean!' said his mother. 'What about you, Issie?'

'I'll have the same.'

'The same? You don't have to have what he does.'

Isabella knew that. 'I like hot peas in vinegar,' she said.

Mrs Flynn gave them extra-large portions but they only had to pay the basic amount. The owner sat at the till watching with hawk eyes.

Halfway along the street they ran into Arthur. He was with another lad, taller even than Arthur, who was a good height himself at almost six feet. Arthur's friend held himself well. Somehow you couldn't imagine him eating a bag of chips or peas in the street, or anywhere else for that matter. He looked two or three years older than Arthur. He was wearing a suit with a crisp white shirt and a red and black striped tie. Isabella realised that she was staring at him and dropped her gaze. You didn't see many young men dressed like that around the East End. Go into the City and then you would.

Arthur was looking slightly embarrassed. 'Rupert,' he said hesitantly, 'this is my sister, Isabella.'

'Pleased to meet you, Isabella,' said Rupert inclining his head in her direction. He smiled at her, engaging her eyes, and she dropped her gaze. She didn't know why but he made her feel uncomfortable.

'This is Sean,' she said hurriedly. It was obvious that Arthur was not going to introduce him. Compared with Rupert or Arthur, he looked – well, Isabella had to admit it – a bit scruffy, in baggy old corduroy trousers and a navy blue jumper, frayed around the neck and the cuffs. The Flynns had so little money they had to shop in second-hand clothes shops and pawn shops, something Arthur would never do. He'd always been fussy about his clothes. He saved something from his wages each week so that he could buy new ones.

Rupert nodded his head in Sean's direction.

'Fancy a couple of peas?' Sean stuck his bag under Rupert's nose.

Rupert leaned backwards to avoid the smell. Arthur stared at his feet. Isabella was troubled. What was going on with him these days? He'd been such a nice, kind boy when he was younger, keen to please. They'd been good friends, though not as close as she was with William. Arthur was easily influenced, and always had been. He'd got in with the wrong crowd now, she felt sure of that. He was spending more money. He'd asked her for a loan only a few days ago and she'd given him three shillings out of her money box and told him that was all she could afford. She earned less than he did.

'We'd best be getting along, Arthur,' said Rupert.

'Ta-ra,' said Sean.

'Bye,' said Isabella.

'Goodnight,' said Rupert.

They parted.

'Goodnight!' said Sean, imitating Rupert's smooth voice. 'Who does he think he is? Lord Muck?'

Arthur and his friend had made for the nearest bus stop. Isabella hovered until she saw them get on a bus. It was going to Oxford Street. The only time she went there was with Bridie to look in the shop windows.

'Twerp!' exclaimed Sean. 'I felt like punching him in the nose.'

'Well, don't bother! We've enough trouble going on.'

'He'd better stay off our patch. Else I'll give him what for! Don't know what your Arthur's doin' with an eejit like him. Didn't like the way he looked at you either.'

'What's it to you?'

Sean crumpled up his empty bag and tossed it into a bin. Isabella smiled. He took her hand and they swung arms between them as they carried on down the street.

Six

For once they had something to look forward to. Isabella was excited. She and her mother had been invited to dance at the Queen's Theatre in Poplar on Saturday night. Her mother was a brilliant flamenco dancer and had taught Isabella to dance, almost since she could walk, in the way that her own mother had taught her.

Normally they played only in small venues but one of the performers at the Queen's had fallen ill and Isabella and her mother had been asked to fill in for him. It seemed they were becoming known. The theatre could hold more than a thousand people. A thousand! They usually played in halls that might not even take a hundred.

Her mother had laid out their dresses. Hers was predominantly black with red flounces around the neck and hem, whilst Isabella's was red with black flounces. They had been brought from Malaga.

They dressed, helping each other with their costumes and then her mother wound Isabella's hair round her head and secured it with a large black comb and a red rose.

'There!' Maria said, standing back to survey her daughter. 'You look like a true flamenco dancer now, straight from Granada.' She spoke in Spanish. It was as if, in her flamenco dress, she had forgotten she lived in London. She was back in Spain in her head. Isabella understood everything she said and responded in Spanish, even if not so fluently.

When they came downstairs, Jim Blake whistled. 'Magnificent!' He clapped his hands flamenco-style. 'You will bowl the crowd over.'

'We will dance for William,' said his wife.

The two dancers put coats over their dresses and they set out. Even so, with the roses in their hair and frills around their ankles, they were bound to attract attention. Heads turned.

Isabella felt happy for the first time since William had left. It seemed as if he'd been away for months but it was only four weeks. She wished he could be there tonight to see them dance but he could not and so she thought only of the performance ahead. The rhythm of the flamenco music was in her head. She tapped her toe in time with it while they waited for the tram. Her mother was smiling, her worries forgotten for the moment.

When they reached the theatre they saw that people were already lining up outside.

'Look, Mama!' cried Isabella.

The queue stretched right along the pavement and more people were joining it every minute. Street performers were entertaining them while they waited. Accordion players. Penny whistlers doing a little jog while they piped. Tap dancers. Boys with mouth organs. Anyone who could play anything that was portable seemed to be there. Singers too. One man was warbling 'Molly Malone', his hand placed dramatically over his chest as if his heart was broken. The song was Bridie's mother's favourite. *In Dublin's fair city, where the girls are so pretty, I first set my eyes on sweet Molly Malone.* She could often be heard singing it as she came along the street, especially if she'd called in at the pub and had had a half of Guinness. Or, if she was lucky and someone had bought it for her, a shot of gin with peppermint.

Bridie had promised to come to their show tonight with Sean. And there they were, halfway up the queue, waving. Isabella waved back.

Some of the entertainers had friends with them who worked the queue, holding out a tin lid or a bowl, hoping for contributions. A penny here, a ha'penny there. Anything, even a farthing, was welcomed. Those who were on their own stopped for a few minutes to do their own touting, the men doffing their caps in thanks. There was a general feeling of gaiety in the air and, across the street, on the edge of the pavement, sat a line of small kids enjoying the show, sucking lollipops or eating pokes of chips. Saturday night was a night out for everybody.

'Isn't it great, Mama?'

'*Excelente! Olé!*' Isabella's mother clicked her hands above her head, making the people in the queue laugh and smile.

Isabella stood up on her toes to get a better look at the head of the queue. She frowned.

'What is it, love?'

'Nothing, Mama.'

Yes, it was definitely Arthur's friend Rupert! Isabella recognised his sleek hair and the way he held his head. He was taller than most men in the crowd so he stood out. The inhabitants of the East End were not noted for their height.

Rupert was with a friend, though it was not Arthur. She didn't quite know why, but something about him unsettled her. When she looked again, he and his companion were walking up and down, chatting to people in the queue, which surprised her. They appeared to be handing out pieces of paper. Surely not tickets? Leaflets, possibly.

'Isabella,' said her mother. 'I think it is time we went in.'

'I think so too,' said her father. 'Good luck!'

He already had a ticket so he was able to walk on up ahead and skirt the queue. Isabella and her mother made for the performers' entrance.

The stage door! Isabella had never imagined coming in through a real stage door along with the other performers. The dressing rooms were full. Isabella and her mother found chairs and sat watching the other women changing and listening to their chatter. They laughed a lot. They mostly seemed to know one another but they greeted the flamenco dancers in a friendly manner and admired their costumes. In the distance they could hear laughter and applause coming from the auditorium and once or twice the sound of booing.

'The audience don't put up with no rubbish,' one of the dressers told them. 'If they don't like you they'll let you know.'

'Oh, Mama,' said Isabella, 'I hope we will be good enough.'

'Of course we will!' Her mother was full of fire.

And then came their turn. They rose when their names were called and followed the stagehand to the wings at the side of the stage. He cautioned them to stay back and then, when it was time, he motioned to them to go forward. The master of ceremonies was out there, standing at the very front of the stage.

'I now give you the fabulous flamenco dancers, mother and daughter, Maria and Isabella, all the way from Malaga in the south of Spain!' he announced. 'Give them a big hand, ladies and gentlemen!'

The audience complied with gusto and when the cheers had died down a guitarist, seated at the side of the stage, struck a chord. They'd had a short practice with him the day before. He was a Spaniard, originally from Granada.

Maria led the way, stepping out confidently, her head thrown back, her hands parked on either side of her hips. Isabella blinked as she came under the lights. They were startlingly bright. The lights over the audience were dimmed, then the guitarist started to play, and Maria and Isabella began to dance. Once they had started Isabella forgot about the audience. She became lost in the movement and the music which powered them on.

When they made their last dramatic turn and the guitarist struck his last note and shouted '*Olé!*' the audience was completely still for a moment and then it erupted. They cheered and stamped their feet. The performers linked hands and bowed and bowed again. Finally, the lights went on in the house so that they could see the rows of faces gazing up at them. Isabella noticed Sean towards the back, on his feet and clapping his hands above his head. Beyond him she saw Rupert standing at the very back near the exit. Even at such a distance, she sensed that he was staring hard at her. She shifted her gaze until she found her father, on his feet too. Most of the audience was standing by now. The applause lasted five minutes.

'*Encore!*' they shouted.

Isabella's mother engaged her eyes and nodded. They raised their arms above their heads. The music began and they began to dance again.

When they were finally released and had retreated to the dressing room they collapsed on to their chairs, utterly exhausted. A dresser passed them towels to dry their faces.

'You fair knocked them out good and proper!' she said.

The manager sent word that he wanted to see them and when they went to his office he said that they had been such a hit he wished to book them in for another performance.

'Four weeks tonight?'

'Very well,' agreed Maria. 'We are very pleased you are happy with us.'

'Indeed I am. Very happy. And so was the audience.'

He also paid them slightly more than the agreed fee.

Isabella's father was waiting for them outside the stage door with Bridie and Sean.

'You did yourselves proud,' he said, giving each of them a hug.

'I think we go home by cab now,' declared Maria. 'We have money. The cabs, they carry five, do they not?'

'They do,' said her husband, taking her arm.

The others walked behind, with Isabella in the middle linking arms with Bridie and Sean, her two best friends. Apart from William, of course. But even with her brother sitting forever at the back of her mind, she felt happy tonight.

Seven

The following afternoon Bridie called in for Isabella. Her four older brothers were away playing in a Gaelic football match. No one knew what Mickey was up to.

'What shall we do?' asked Bridie.

The street was quiet. It had that Sunday feel to it as if half the occupants were asleep beside the fire, which they probably were. Bridie's dad would be. He spent Saturday nights drinking in the pub and slept it off on Sunday. Isabella had an idea circulating in her head. It had come to her first thing that morning when she'd wakened. Before she'd gone to sleep she'd been thinking about Arthur's friend Rupert and the way he had stared at her at the Queen's Theatre. It was not a very pleasant image to go to sleep with when she could have been remembering the cheering crowd in the auditorium and how Sean had stood up at the back of the hall, clapping and smiling. Funny how some things, bad things, mostly, hung on in your head. Now she intended to do something about it.

'Bridie,' she said, pulling on her coat. 'I want to go back over to Poplar. To the High Street.'

'What are you wanting to do for that for? The Queen's will be shut up. There'll be nobody there.'

'I know that. Trust me. Just come. I'll pay your fare.'

Poplar High Street, when they reached it, was no busier than the streets running off Mile End had been.

'Now what?' asked Bridie, as they stood outside the shuttered theatre. Last night's posters looked as if they might have been there for weeks.

'I want to have a look in some of the rubbish bins,' said Isabella.

'Rubbish bins? Whatever for?'

'Never mind. Just a hunch. Look, there's one over there.'

Isabella led the way across the street. Bridie followed, shaking her head. She didn't know what got into Isabella at times.

The bin was full to the brim with abandoned chip papers and sweet wrappers, tins and bottles, and various other bits of rubbish left over from the night before. You wouldn't want to know what some of it was!

'You're never going to stick your hands into that lot!' The idea horrified Bridie.

'Watch me!'

'I ain't helpin', Issie, not with that. Somebody might have puked in it for all you know.'

Isabella ignored Bridie's warning and pulled a strong brown paper grocer's bag out of her pocket. She then tucked her hand into it so that it acted like a glove. Bridie watched incredulously while her friend raked about amongst the rubbish, tossing cans and bottles out on to the ground.

'What are you looking for anyway?'

'Wait and see.' Isabella withdrew her hand finally. No luck here. She frowned. Her makeshift glove was sodden and filthy. She dumped it alongside the other rubbish. She'd have to leave the whole lot lying there. She felt bad about doing that but she couldn't possibly pick it all up with her bare hands. She might cut them on broken glass. A couple of cats were snuffling around the mess already. She considered her next move. She looked up the street. 'See any more bins, Bridie?'

Bridie had sharp eyesight. Isabella's was not so good since she'd started working at Mr Goldberg's sweatshop. It was the dust from the chalk that did it.

'There's one a bit further up,' said Bridie.

'Come on then! Let's go!'

Isabella sprinted off. Bridie had to run to keep up with her. When they reached the other bin, Isabella pulled up sharply and straight away seized a piece of crumpled paper lying just below the rim. She held it aloft and raised a cheer.

'What is it?' asked Bridie.

'Wait a minute and I'll be able to tell you for sure!' Isabella was straightening out the paper. She nodded, then laughed triumphantly. 'I thought I might find one! You see, Bridie, when somebody hands out leaflets half the people that get them chuck them in the nearest bin on their way home. I've done it myself.'

'So have I.'

'You see!'

Bridie still looked puzzled.

'Last night Rupert was handing out leaflets to people in the queue. And this is one of them!'

'What's it about?' Bridie angled her head to look.

'A meeting.'

'What kind of meeting?'

'Political.'

'Political?'

'For young people interested in Mr Oswald Mosley. It's inviting you to come along and hear all about the British Union of Fascists and what they really stand for.'

'And what do they?'

'*The good of our country*, so they say. England for the English! That means not you. Or my mum. She's Spanish. Or Mr Goldberg. He's Jewish.'

'But I was born here!' retorted Bridie.

'Your mum and dad weren't though, were they? They're Irish. Some people don't like you being here.'

'What harm did we ever do to anybody?'

'If we went into the meeting we might find out.'

'We're not goin', are we?' Bridie was alarmed.

'It says that too many foreigners are coming into our country,' said Isabella, reading from the leaflet.

'They're a nasty lot, them Fascists.'

'They are.' Isabella waved the piece of crumpled paper aloft. 'This is Arthur's friend Rupert trying to recruit people for the cause. I saw him last night. That's what it's all about. There'll probably be a few more of these lying around.' She tucked the leaflet into her pocket. She was even more worried now about Arthur, but she didn't want to talk about it to Bridie before she was sure, not yet anyway. And she might be wrong.

They retraced their steps back down the street passing the locked-up theatre that last night had rocked with fun and laughter. Isabella pulled the leaflet back out of her pocket and checked the details.

'Meeting's at seven tonight. In a hall in Balham.'

'You're not really thinking of goin'?' asked Bridie. 'Seriously, Issie?'

She knew what Isabella was like, how she could be fiery and not hesitate to get involved in an argument when she disagreed with what was going on. Bridie didn't fancy going to a meeting where Isabella might get up and heckle the speaker.

'Not exactly,' said Isabella. 'Not to the meeting itself. I'd just like to go along tonight and see who's there.'

'You're not wanting to get yourself mixed up with the likes of them though, are you?'

'Course not. I've no intention of getting mixed up with them.'

Bridie asked no further questions. She'd had enough of politics and people fighting over them. 'Let's go into town and have a look at the shops.'

'All right.' Isabella enjoyed a walk down Oxford Street herself. The shops wouldn't be open, not on a Sunday, of course, but that didn't matter. They couldn't afford to buy anything in them anyway.

They did their window shopping and Bridie chattered all the way home about the clothes they'd seen. 'Wouldn't it be great to be able to buy one of those frocks in Selfridges? I liked that blue one with the Peter Pan collar.'

Isabella, who would have fancied buying a dress herself, though not that particular one, said, 'Maybe one day!'

'We'd need to find us a couple of rich fellas.'

Isabella didn't reply. She was thinking about something else right now.

'Not likely though, is it?' Bridie laughed.

'What?'

'Us finding rich fellas in the East End. Mind you, you might get to become a star with your dancing. You might play in the West End.'

'I doubt it,' said Isabella.

Isabella rapped on Bridie's door just after six o'clock.

'Come away in,' said Mrs Flynn. 'We've just had our tea.'

Bridie was finishing the dishes and all the boys were out except for Sean, who was cleaning his football boots. He was a talented footballer and people said he might play for one of the big London clubs one of these days. Like Arsenal or Tottenham.

'You've got to be jokin',' he'd say when anyone suggested it.

'Any news of your William, Issie?' asked Mrs Flynn.

'Not yet. It takes a while for letters to come from Spain.' And they didn't even know if William would have a chance to send one after he'd crossed the border. Recent news from Spain had been about violent clashes between Republicans and Nationalists. The latter were better armed, due to help from Germany and Italy. The Republicans had asked for similar support from London but it seemed that Britain didn't want to be involved.

'Where are you off to, the two of you?' asked Sean, changing the conversation.

'Issie's got a bee in her bonnet,' announced Bridie.

'Oh?' said Sean. 'Another?'

He ducked when Isabella slanted a punch at him.

'So what is it?' he asked

Isabella didn't want to say anything in front of Mr and Mrs Flynn. Bridie's dad was dozing in his armchair but his wife was not. Mrs Flynn liked any titbit of gossip that came her way. On sunny days she would stand at her door, leaning against the jamb, cigarette in the corner of her mouth, and ask passers-by if there was anything new going around. Isabella's mother had advised her not to tell Mrs Flynn anything unless she wanted it broadcast all along the street.

'Where are youse off to then?' she asked the girls and winked. 'Meetin' any boys?'

Sean perked up his head at that.

'Oh, look at our Sean!' said his mother. 'He didn't like that idea. Did you, son?' she added.

She didn't get an answer. He was frowning. Isabella smiled.

'We thought we'd take a walk along Oxford Street,' put in Bridie. 'Have a wee look in the shop windows.'

'That'd be nice,' said her mother.

'I thought you went there this afternoon?' said Sean.

Bridie ignored that. She dried her hands and put on her coat.

'I'll keep you company to the bus stop,' offered Sean.

Once outside, Isabella told him about Rupert and the leaflets. She showed him the crumpled one that she'd carried round all day.

'You're not going to the meeting, are you?'

'No, I'm just curious to see who's there.'

'In that case, I'm comin' with you. I had a feeling you were up to something, the two of youse.'

It was beginning to get dark by the time they reached Balham and found the hall. All the better, thought Isabella, for then they wouldn't be so noticeable. They approached the place cautiously and walked past without stopping, Sean and Bridie following Isabella's lead. Pinned to the door was a notice which said: *Youth Club tonight 7pm. All welcome.*

'Youth Club?' queried Bridie.

'They can call it anything they want,' said Isabella.

A boy standing on the pavement outside held out a leaflet and invited the girls to come and join them.

'We've got some great speakers. Why not come in and hear them?'

Isabella shook her head and they carried on. The boy was no longer interested in them, he had turned his attention to another couple of lads, who had stopped and were listening with bent heads. They went into the hall.

'Let's cross the road, watch from there,' said Isabella.

They found a shop doorway to take shelter in.

'This is exciting,' said Bridie. 'It's like that Sherlock Holmes you get out the library.'

'Except that there's no crime,' said Isabella. But there was something she needed to solve.

'What are we doin' here anyway?' asked Sean. 'If we're not goin' in.'

'Wait!' replied Isabella.

A few more young people were going into the hall, not many, no more than a dozen, mainly boys, and a couple of girls.

'There's that friend of Arthur's!' exclaimed Bridie.

Rupert had just come out of the hall and was glancing up and down the street as if he were looking for more recruits to rope in. He wore grey trousers and a loose black fencing top with a thick leather belt round his waist.

'He's a Blackshirt right enough, dressed like that,' murmured Sean. 'A Mosley man.'

The three in the doorway shrank back as far as they could. Isabella didn't think Rupert had noticed them. It was getting dark and he was watching his own side of the street. He had his eye on two girls walking arm in arm coming up the street. They stopped and he began to talk to them. He inclined his head, bringing it down to their level, and he gesticulated, moving his hands about. He touched one girl on the arm, then the other.

'He knows every trick,' observed Sean.

'Don't go in, girls,' murmured Isabella.

But they did. Rupert shepherded them in, keeping a hand on each of their backs until they were through the doorway.

'He must have charmed them,' commented Bridie.

'Idiots!' said Isabella.

A few seconds later Rupert came out to take a last quick look around and then went back inside. The three watchers hung around for a few more minutes but there was no further action in the street. They were just about to move on when they saw the doors across the street burst open and a boy come flying out on to the pavement. He staggered, trying to get his balance. Two heavy-looking men dressed in overalls followed behind him.

'Don't show your face in here again, mate,' shouted one. 'You might land in the river next time.' They retreated inside, laughing.

Sean started to cross the road to go and help the boy when Isabella hissed, 'Hang on a minute. Somebody's coming out to close the doors.'

'Look! It's your Arthur, Issie!' cried Bridie.

Eight

That was just what Isabella had been afraid of, that she might see her brother here.

'Your dad would have a fit if he thought Arthur was mixed up with that lot,' said Bridie.

'You're telling me!' agreed Isabella. She must try to make sure that her father didn't find out. She could only hope Arthur would come to his senses without getting too far in. But perhaps he was already! The thought made her feel sick.

They hung around for a while. The boy who'd been kicked out had managed to get to his feet and take off. The street was quiet now. There was little action except for a couple of cats having a scrap. A wind had sprung up.

Bridie shivered and pulled up her coat collar. A man came by but he walked straight on past the hall without giving it a glance. Isabella wished she could be in there like a fly on the wall.

It was getting darker and colder. 'Let's go!' Isabella said abruptly. She wanted to get away from the place.

'Yes, let's,' said Sean.

'I'm freezin',' said Bridie.

But Isabella was still not moving. There was something keeping her there.

'Do you know,' said Sean, 'I can't really believe your Arthur would be such an eejit as to get mixed up with a crowd like that, Issie.'

The trouble was Isabella could. Arthur was far too easily impressed, especially by people who had money.

Suddenly Sean hissed, 'Wait!'

The door of the hall had opened again and a shaft of light spilled on to the pavement. Out came the two heavy-looking men. This time they were dragging a boy behind them by the scruff of his neck. Isabella held her breath. The men flung the boy across the pavement, dusted off their hands and went back inside. Arthur then came out to close the double doors again.

'Must have been a heckler,' said Sean. 'Seems like Arthur is being used as a bouncer, him being so strong.'

But Isabella wasn't listening, she was already running towards the boy, who was lying where he had been thrown, in the gutter. Sean followed on her heels. By the time they reached the boy he had managed to scramble up on to his knees.

'Are you all right?' asked Sean.

'Aye.' He touched the back of his head and groaned.

'I'm sorry,' Isabella started to say, then stopped. She couldn't apologise for her brother. She wished she could bang on the doors and demand that Arthur come out here but she knew that would not be a good idea. He wouldn't hit her, she wasn't afraid of that. Their father would go berserk if he did. It was Rupert that she feared. There was something menacing in his cold eyes.

'Are you all right, mate?' asked Sean.

'Yeah. Wait till I git my hands on them!' The boy glanced back at the closed doors and raised a clenched fist in the air. He'd get nowhere with that, of course, though neither Isabella nor Sean would tell him so. The very thought of Arthur being involved in such an outfit made Isabella fume inside.

'You've got blood on your forehead.' She frowned. She took a hanky out of her pocket and dabbed the boy's temple. Fortunately it was only a slight graze, but it left a streak of blood on the lace-edged handkerchief given to her by Sean for her birthday. She shoved it into her pocket before he could see it.

'Hey,' said the boy, looking at Sean, 'I know you, don't I? I've seen you somewhere. At the march?'

'I was there right enough.'

'Did you not help one of our pals when he got knocked down by a police horse?'

'Robbie?' Sean nodded.

'That's him! How's he doing, do you know? We haven't set eyes on him since then.'

They were silent for a moment, then Isabella blurted out, 'He's dead!'

'Dead? Robbie? He can't be –'

'He is,' said Isabella miserably. 'We did what we could but . . .' She shook her head. She told him how her mother had nursed Robbie until he'd been taken to hospital. 'They couldn't save him.'

'Did you know him well like?' asked Sean. 'The lad?'

'Only for a few days,' said the boy. 'We were dossing down in the same place.'

'We're trying to find his home address,' said Isabella. 'So we could let his family know.'

'Can't help you there. Some of the other lads might have an idea.' He got to his feet. 'You can come back with me now if you want. They call me Jackie, by the way.' He held out his hand.

The girls and Sean introduced themselves. Jackie took a quick look back at the hall doors, shouted, 'Scum!' and then they set off.

Jackie was living – if it could be called that – down near the East Dock. He and four other boys were encamped in an abandoned warehouse. The place smelled of rot and the roof was half caved in. The only light was from a lantern set on the floor and the flickering of a fire in an oil drum. Four boys were seated round the drum when they arrived. Mick. Gerry. Abe. Archie. Jackie pointed to each in turn and told them how he had met the three visitors.

'Told you it were a waste of time going to that meeting,' said Mick. 'One heckle and you're out.'

'Take a pew,' invited Abe.

The girls were wearing their best coats, it being Sunday. Isabella hesitated for only a second, then sat down on the dirty concrete floor. Bridie followed suit and Sean joined them.

The boys were passing a bottle of beer round the circle. The newcomers shook their heads when it was offered, which was probably a relief to the boys.

'Live round here?' asked Abe.

'Off the Mile End Road,' answered Sean.

'Got any dough?' asked Gerry. 'We ain't eaten all day.'

Sean took a shilling out of his pocket. 'Sorry, that's all I've got.'

'It'll buy us a cup of tea in the morning. What about you, sweetheart?' Gerry turned to Isabella.

She rummaged in her pocket and found a sixpence.

'That all?'

'I've got tuppence,' offered Bridie. 'Oh, and here's a ha'penny.'

'Any offerings gratefully received.' Gerry put the coins in his pocket.

Bridie sat close to Isabella. They were glad that Sean was with them. The boys were probably all right, but the place was a bit scary and made Isabella think of a scene in one of Charles Dickens's books, she couldn't think which. Her dad had introduced them to her. He read a lot. He'd started taking her to the library when she was small. He was a man who valued education and wished he'd had a chance to learn more. He went to Workers Educational classes doggedly every week, even when he was tired.

Jackie was telling his friends what had happened to Robbie.

'Poor sod,' said Gerry. 'The police should get done for that.'

'Fat chance,' said Mick.

Isabella asked if any of them knew anything about Robbie. He'd come from Glasgow, that was all they knew.

'Just a minute,' said Archie. 'He had a pal called Sandy. Think he came from Glasgow too.'

'Do you know where we could find Sandy?'

'He's around. I'll try and track him down.'

'Would you? That'd be great. We could come back tomorrow.'

'Give us your address and I'll come by and let you know if I find anything.'

'Fancy her, do you then, Archie?' Gerry had a ghoulish grin but perhaps in the weird flickering light they all looked like ghouls.

'Shut your mouth!' snapped Archie.

There came a rattle like pebbles falling on what remained of the roof. The rain was light to start with, gradually turning heavier. Puddles quickly formed on the shed floor. They were fine though by the fire. In fact it felt quite cosy to be sitting there watching the flames, listening to the rain falling. Isabella began to feel a little woozy, even hypnotised.

They were roused by the sudden arrival of a dark, burly figure wearing a cape. The lads groaned. The policeman was no stranger to them. He took off his helmet, shook off the raindrops, then put it back on his head. 'Still here then, are you?'

'Looks like it,' said Archie.

'I thought you were moving on?'

'Tomorrow,' said Gerry.

'It's always tomorrow for you boys. You can't stay here indefinitely, you know. I should move you on now.'

'You wouldn't do that to us, would you, Constable?' said Archie. 'Put us out in the cold? Anyway, we ain't doin' no harm to nobody.'

The constable shook his head and moved up closer to the fire himself. It was only then that he noticed Sean and the girls.

'And where have you lot come from?''

'Jumped out the sky,' said Archie, grinning.

'We're just going.' Sean got to his feet. To Archie he said, 'We'll come round again tomorrow night and see if you managed to find out anything about Robbie. Come on then, girls.'

'Pay us a visit any time, girls,' Gerry called after them. 'But leave your minder behind.' He winked at Bridie, who tossed her head at him.

'Silly twerp,' she said underneath her breath.

Isabella resisted the urge to brush the dirt off her coat when she stood up. She'd do it outside, before she got home and her mother's sharp eyes saw it. She'd only had it a month and it was a light greyish-blue. It would show up the dirt, her mother had said when Isabella chose it. Navy blue would have been more sensible.

'You might bring us some grub when you come,' Gerry called after them.

'We'll see what we can do,' said Sean.

'Got a job, have you?' asked Archie.

'In the yard.'

'Lucky you.' There was no mistaking the sarcastic tone in his voice.

Not that lucky for Sean, thought Isabella, slogging away in the docks, but she didn't say so. She didn't want to start an argy-bargy with this bunch. Sean was looking tensed, as if he'd like to spring on Archie.

'Time you started working for your living too, you lot,' said the constable to the boys, while warming his hands by the fire. He seemed quite at home, in no hurry to leave. It was cold outside.

Jackie walked a little way with Sean and the girls.

'I'm getting out of here soon as I can,' he told them. 'Heading back up north. Me mum lives in Newcastle.'

'If I was you I would,' said Bridie. 'You'll get your death living in that dump.'

They said goodbye to Jackie and set off. They had no money for the tram now. It was going to be a long wet walk.

'Don't suppose they'll find anything out,' said Sean. 'About Robbie, I mean. But it's worth a chance. I don't want either of you going back there on your own,' he added.

Nine

The days were shortening and temperatures dropping. There was no heating on in Goldberg's workroom but once they got going there was enough warmth given off by the bodies of the ten women to keep them sweating. Sweatshop was a good name for workshops like this one. The harder they worked the more they sweated and the more they earned. The women's feet flew over the treadles powering the machines while their hands guided the material under the needles as the sharp points darted up and down. Isabella's eyes itched even more today from the dust and the tailor's chalk and she was finding it difficult to concentrate. It had been some time now since the march and she'd been thinking about Robbie again and his mum up in Glasgow waiting for news. If he had a mum.

'Pay attention, Isabella!' snapped Mr Glump, their supervisor. 'That seam is not straight. You'll have to unpick it.'

She sighed. He was right. She could see that herself. People paid good money to have their clothes made. They wanted well-made garments. Goldberg's was considered to be one of the better tailors in the East End. Christmas orders kept coming in so at least they knew there'd be work up to the end of the year. Her dad said the recession was affecting everybody, even the well-off ones from places like the West End and Hampstead.

'Sorry, Mr Glump,' she said and set to work.

'So am I.'

Mr Glump was not popular with the workers. How could he be when his job was to find fault and see that there was no slacking? It didn't help, either, that he often smelled of grease and his scruffy beard often had bits of food caught in it. One of the women who lived next door to him claimed that neither he nor his wife ever went near the public baths. And, as she said, you couldn't imagine him sitting in a tin bath in front of the fire washing himself. He was too fat!

Isabella and Bridie went to the public baths together twice a week and Isabella's mother made sure the boys did too. She thought of Will. Where did you wash if you were fighting a war? Maybe it didn't matter if you smelled then, though Isabella was sure Will would always find a pond or a stream. She studied the piece of material in front of her. It was slippery moss-green taffeta that she had to transform into a ball gown for a woman who lived in Berkeley Square. Mrs Cranford-Smythe was a woman who was hard to please but she was a good customer. She had to be pampered. Mr Glump fawned over her and even Mr Goldberg emerged from his office to greet her, which he didn't do for every customer. He was not always on the premises. He did all the purchasing of the materials and when he was out Mr Glump acted as if he were the owner, swanning about and finding fault. Isabella longed for the day when she would be able to walk into the sweatshop, hand Mr Glump her notice and inform him that she was going to work as a stenographer. In a clean warm office. In the City.

'Get moving, girl!' He poked her in the back with a sharp knuckle. 'You're not paid to sit here and doze.'

She went back to work. Her hands kept slipping on the material.

Arthur hadn't come in until late last night. She hadn't been able to get to sleep. Thoughts of Will had kept her awake too. During the day she tried not to think of him, but at night it was different, lying in the dark listening to the faint rumble of traffic out in the street. She had heard Arthur open the front door and pause. He would have been taking off his shoes and stopping to find out if anyone had heard him. He then began to climb the stairs. The third one creaked. He should know to avoid it.

'Arthur?' Their mother seldom slept until they were all home.

'Yes, Mother.'

'Where have you been?'

'Out with the lads.'

'Which lads are they?'

'You don't know them.'

'Drinking, were you? Not too much, I hope?'

'No, Mother.'

'Go to bed then. You will be so tired for the work I will not be able to wake you and then you get sack!'

It was fortunate that their father tended to sleep soundly. Their mother said if a bomb was falling she would have to waken him.

Isabella didn't want to think about bombs. They led her to picturing Will cowering under a makeshift shelter, Italian planes screeching overhead, diving low, ready to drop their deadly loads.

ॐ

There were two letters from abroad lying on the table that day when Isabella came in from work, exhausted. One of the stamps was French and the other Spanish. Her heart thumped.

'William?' she asked eagerly.

'Yes,' said her mother, smiling, 'from William! And my sister Cecilia.'

William had taken a bundle of plain postcards and envelopes with him in case he had a chance to send one from time to time. Isabella took the postcard from her mother's outstretched hand and began to read.

I write to let you know I am fit and well. We are close to the border waiting to cross into Spain. Some nice ladies came to meet our train and wish us well. They brought food and wine and one of them, Marguerite, has kindly offered to post this for me. I hope it will reach you. Please do not worry about me. I will write again whenever possible.
Your loving son,
William.

'But that must have been written a while ago,' cried Isabella.

So the card was out of date. By now William must be over the border and could well be in the thick of the Spanish civil war. In spite of that their mother looked relieved. Every night she prayed to Mary Mother of God to protect him and now she held a letter from her son in her hand.

Isabella felt only frustration. What good was an out-of-date postcard?

Her mother translated the second letter as she read it

aloud. Cecilia and her family had fled from Malaga along the coast with the other evacuees, as they had imagined they might.

It was terrible when the planes appeared in the sky. We knew then we must go. We had to take only what we could carry and leave the rest. We had to move quickly. Guido scavenged and found a small handcart. It had one wheel missing but we were able to push it along with some bedding and clothes in it. The children were very good. They did as they were told and carried what they could. They were very quiet.

But, Maria, we have lost our home and everything in it! Can you imagine? The planes went on bombing us even as we were leaving. Italian planes, sent by Mussolini. They flew low. We could see their faces. They must have seen ours. We had to take shelter behind a broken-down wall.

'It is terrible!' Isabella's mother wept, unable to read on.

Isabella wiped a few tears from her eyes too. It was difficult to imagine your life changing so quickly. One minute you have a home, the next minute you're trudging along the road pushing your belongings in an old handcart. If the war with Germany that everyone was worrying about were to happen, would they have to leave their homes and trek along the coast or go north to

Scotland? But planes can go anywhere. They can follow you. They have the whole width of the sky to move about in. The people beneath them have only streets or open fields. It was crazy, all of it. Their next-door neighbours, the Manns, were German. They were good friends. They didn't want to fight them. They came in some evenings to have a game of cards with her mum and dad. Isabella's head rocked with so many thoughts swirling through it.

'Where are they now?' she asked. 'Aunt Cecilia and the family?'

'In a small fishing village called Nerja. But Cecilia says it is a poor place and she doesn't know how they can earn money. She thinks the fishermen barely make enough to feed themselves and their families.'

Isabella wondered how her aunt had managed to send the letter but it seemed that an American journalist covering the war for his newspaper back home had come to the fishing village on his way north to France and offered to take letters and post them for anyone who wanted to send word to friends and relatives.

'They are sleeping in a makeshift shack on the beach,' said her mother. 'I wish I could bring them to London.'

They both knew there was no hope of that.

Her mother folded the letter and put it back in its envelope. Isabella gave her a hug and they clung to each other for a few minutes. Then her mother sighed and said life had to go on.

'Take Arthur's laundry up for me, would you, love?'

Isabella lifted the pile of freshly ironed shirts and pyjamas and carried them upstairs. Arthur's room was tidy, the bed well made. Isabella laid his laundry on the bed and closed the door quietly behind her. She knew it was wrong to poke into other people's belongings but she was sorely tempted. Gingerly she opened the top drawer of the chest: it held Arthur's socks neatly rolled, the next one his underwear. She was about to close the drawer when she glimpsed something in the bottom of it. She lifted the underwear and looked underneath. It was an armband bearing the BUF's symbol: a white lightning flash set inside a blue circle against a red background. A chill swept through her. This was what she had feared.

She heard the front door opening and her dad calling out, 'I'm home, Maria.' Isabella quickly replaced the armband and closed the drawer. Then she ran down the stairs.

The first thing her dad did when he came in from work was to turn on the wireless to listen to the news. This evening there was a report about fierce fighting on the outskirts of Madrid. It appeared that some members of the International Brigades were involved and amongst them were some British.

'Casualties are reported to be high on both sides,' said the announcer.

'It doesn't necessarily mean William will be there, does

it?' asked Isabella desperately. 'It's a big country, Spain, isn't it? Bigger than England and Scotland put together. You've said that yourself, Dad. Will could be anywhere.'

Neither of her parents responded.

Arthur, who had just come in and heard the tail end of the news, said he wasn't hungry and walked out, slamming the door behind him.

'You see,' said their mother, 'he does care about William. I can tell! Even though they fight. They are brothers after all.'

Ten

Isabella tossed and turned in her bed and couldn't settle down. There was something wrong. The room felt stuffy. She opened the front window to get a breath of air. And then she smelled burning.

She went into the hall and yelled up the stairs. 'Dad, come down! Quickly!'

'What is it?' he asked as he came running down, tying the cord of his dressing gown.

'Can you smell burning?'

'Certainly can!'

They went out on to the pavement. They saw flames in the sky.

'It's not far away, Issie. Go inside! I'm going to put some clothes on and see what's going on.'

'I'm coming with you,' she said and grabbed her coat and shoes.

She stood at the open door waiting for her dad. The smell was getting stronger. When he reappeared, they began to run towards the seat of the fire. By now the smoke was catching at their throats and making them double over with coughing. A fire engine came roaring up behind them and went sailing past, its siren wailing. And then came another. People were running. They were all headed in the same direction.

They were joined by Sean and Bridie coming up behind them. The flames in the sky were clearer now, orange and red and black. Isabella thought she was going to choke.

'Must be a humdinger,' cried Sean, as they rushed on.

They turned a corner and gasped. A building was on fire. It was Goldberg's!

The tailor's workshop was alight from top to bottom. Anyone could see straight away that there would be no chance of saving it even though the firemen were plying their hoses with full force. Their only hope would be to try to stop it from spreading. By now the street was full of people, some scurrying, racing frantically to and fro, carrying clothes over their arms or dragging bits and pieces of furniture along the pavement. The police were there, shouting at them to keep back, but they paid little attention. They didn't want to lose what little they had. The fire crackled and spat and fumed. Even from several yards away the heat could be felt.

'Move back, for the love of God!' yelled a fireman. 'You'll end up like toast if you don't.'

This time the crowd moved, all but one man. Mr

Goldberg himself. He stood completely still, staring up into the flames as if hypnotised.

'Poor man,' said Jim Blake. 'His life's work gone.'

'Who'd do a thing like that?' asked Sean.

It wasn't difficult to hazard a guess. Someone who hated Jews.

There had been fires before in the neighbourhood but none that matched the ferocity of the one in front of them. This fire was relentless. A woman, struck in the face by a spark, screamed.

'Let's go home,' said Jim Blake. 'It'll burn all night. There's nothing we can do to help.'

'You're right there, Mr Blake,' said Sean.

They walked back the way they had come without saying a word.

Mrs Flynn was at her door. 'Where's the fire?' she asked.

'Goldberg's,' said Isabella.

'God save us! What's the world coming to?'

Bridie went in and Sean walked Isabella and her dad to their door. The street was still full of people. The menacing orange glow lit up the night sky. Isabella felt sick at the pit of her stomach. She was thinking of Arthur and the armband in his drawer. But surely he wouldn't—?

Her mother was standing on the doorstep in her dressing gown, her long black hair loose around her shoulders.

'Is Arthur in?' asked Isabella.

'He's been in this hour back. Why?'

'Just wondered,' she said lamely.

Her dad gave her an odd look.

'I'd best be going,' said Sean. 'See you the morrow, Issie.'

He left them and Isabella went inside with her father.

'So where was the fire?' asked her mother.

'Goldberg's,' her husband told her. He shook his head. 'They won't be able to save anything.'

'*Madre mia*! Some people along the road had a rock thrown through their window last week. It just missed the baby in his high chair. It could have killed him.'

'I heard,' said Jim Blake. 'They were from Lithuania.'

'Many people, they do not like us to come from other countries.'

'Everyone likes you, Mama,' Isabella reassured her.

'Because I am not a Jew.'

'No!' protested Isabella. 'Not just that.'

No one could dislike her mother. She looked so lovely and was so lively and she smiled at everyone and said '*Hola*!' even to some of the most mean-minded, who were forever griping or criticising someone. She softened them. Also, she was Jim Blake's wife, and that counted. Few wished to tangle with him. Like his son Arthur he had been a first-class boxer in his youth and was tall and well built.

Isabella couldn't get Mr Goldberg out of her head. What would he do now? He most likely would not have been insured. Not many firms round here were. Insuring a commercial property against fire and flood was expensive, though it was false economy, as her father said. Their own house was insured. A man came round from the Prudential Insurance Company – the Pru, as it was known – and their mother gave him a weekly payment, which he entered in their little green book. She said it made her feel secure, just the very sight of it in the drawer of the dresser. Burglary was the main risk. Gas-meter bandits. If they found an unlocked door – the woman of the house might just have nipped out for a minute to the shops or gone to the privvy in the back yard – they would be inside in a flash and hacking open the gas meter and helping themselves to the coins.

'Let's go to bed,' said Jim Blake.

Lying in the semi-dark, with the smell of smoke still tainting her hair, Isabella listened to the usual night-time sounds, which seemed louder than usual. Her mind drifted back again to Arthur. And from him to Rupert. It was obvious that Arthur was very much under the influence of his new friend. She dwelled on Rupert. He might be a bit arrogant and thought himself to be a cut above the others around him, but she couldn't imagine him torching a building and running away. That wouldn't be like him, somehow. He could hold meetings, give speeches, persuade boys like Arthur to follow him. But she couldn't see him setting light to anything. She felt relieved, at least in part.

And then a different thought came to her, one she had been trying to push to the back of her mind. In the morning Goldberg's would be nothing but a burned-out shell. It would no longer be a busy tailor's shop. And she would have no job.

Out of work! The words had such a terrible ring to them. So many people were out of work.

Too exhausted to think any more, Isabella went to sleep and got up at six as usual, as if she were still going to work. It was only when she was sluicing her face with cold water that she remembered. The fire! How could she have forgotten? She rushed through to the kitchen where her mother was putting out porridge for her dad and Arthur. They were both in their work clothes.

'I can't go to work!' she cried and then immediately, thinking of Mr Goldberg, she felt mean. He had lost his business. His livelihood. And he had a wife and five children, with another on the way and no relations in this country to help them. They would be in the poorhouse.

'Did you hear about the fire?' she asked Arthur. 'At Goldberg's?'

'How could I not! I was awake last night when you came in. I heard.'

'Who do you think would do a thing like that?'

Arthur shrugged. 'No idea.'

Isabella turned and looked out of the window. A steady stream of people, men and boys mostly, some girls and women, were going past. On their way to work. She turned back and faced her father. 'What am I going to do?'

'Look for another job, love. You've been going to evening classes – you'll soon find something new.'

'Don't upset yourself so much, child,' said her mother, coming to put an arm round her shoulders. 'We are not going to starve. Your papa and Arthur, they will still bring money home.'

'We don't have William's wage either.'

'But I don't have to feed him. I wish I did,' his mother added in a quiet voice.

Isabella nodded, unable to speak.

Arthur gulped down his last mouthful of tea and got up. 'I'd best be going. Don't want to be late.'

Their father rose from the table too. He gave both his wife and daughter a hug before leaving. To Isabella he said, 'Your mother's right.'

Isabella waited until the street was quieter, then she put on her workday coat and walked along to Goldberg's.

The building was still smoking and giving out some heat though the fire itself had been extinguished.

'Sorry looking sight it is,' said a woman passing with her shopping bag over her arm.

Isabella nodded. Hearing a familiar voice she turned. Mr Goldberg came up to join her. He stood staring at the ruin and shaking his head as if he couldn't believe his eyes. A policeman was with him. The constable had an open notebook in his hand and a pencil poised, ready to take down details.

'How could anyone do this to me?' Mr Goldberg began to weep.

Isabella looked away. She'd have liked to say something to comfort him but she didn't know what. The slave driver, they used to call him. Now he was a broken man who had lost everything. She laid a hand lightly on his arm.

'Savages!' said the constable. 'If I had my way I'd have them strung up!'

'How can I feed my children?' Mr Goldberg appealed to him. 'And my wife? My poor wife!'

'I'm so sorry, Mr Goldberg,' said Isabella.

'Do you have insurance, sir?' asked the constable.

Mr Goldberg shook his head. 'Sadly, no.' He was going to cry again.

'Best come along to the station with me and make a statement.'

Isabella left them and walked further on down the street, stopping at Levey's the tailor's. Mr Levey had a good name as an employer.

The bell jangled over the door when she opened it. Mr

Levey was seated at the front desk. He looked up at her.

'I wondered if you might need any help, Mr Levey?'

'You worked at Goldberg's, didn't you?'

She nodded.

'Bad business that. Terrible! Who will be next?' Himself? He looked at Isabella and shook his head. 'I'm sorry, young lady, but I can't help you. I've got as many workers as I can afford. Times are hard. Less demand.'

Mr Goldberg had had to let two of his staff go recently, in spite of Christmas orders.

'Thanks, anyway,' said Isabella and walked back out into the street.

She tried four more tailors in the course of the morning. It was the same story at each of them. At one she bumped into Lily, who had worked at Goldberg's with her. Lily was looking for work too, as would the rest of the women from their workshop.

'It's hopeless,' declared Lily, as they fell into step.

'We'll just have to try something different.'

'Like what?

'What about Tate and Lyle's, the sugar factory?' suggested Isabella. 'Or Keillor's?' Her mother used to buy their marmalade when she could afford it.

'Factory work!' said Lily. 'Don't fancy that much.'

'We might have to.'

'Rather do house cleaning.'

They parted. Isabella went home.

'Don't worry,' said her mother. 'We will manage very well. We are fortunate to have two men in the house working.'

Isabella did not feel fortunate. What would she do all day? Sit in the house? Walk the streets?

'You can take the sheets to the wash house for me,' said her mother.

When Isabella was pushing the buggy home loaded with the clean washing she suddenly remembered Robbie and the boys at the Docks. The fire had pushed them to the back of her mind.

After lunch she set off for the Docks.

Archie was the only one in the shed. He was sitting beside the dead fire in the oil drum smoking a cigarette. He straightened up when he saw her.

'Come on in, darling,' he said. 'On our own today? Not got that Irish git with you?'

She instinctively took a step back.

'Hey, hey!' he said. 'Don't be runnin' away! I don't bite, you know.'

'I just came to see if anyone had news about Robbie.'

'What you botherin' your head about him fer? He's dead, ain't he?' He took a step towards her and she took another step back and stumbled over a pile of rubbish. He grabbed her arm. 'Steady on now. You're safe with me.'

'Let me go! Please!'

'You're too pretty to let go.'

Enraged, she kicked him sharply in the shins. He howled and lost the grip on her arm. She ran and on the way out bumped into Jackie.

'Are you all right?' He put his hand on her arm now. He looked past her and saw Archie standing in the doorway of the shack. 'You bin bothering her?'

Archie shrugged and slouched back inside.

'I was wondering if you'd heard anything about Robbie?' asked Isabella, wishing Jackie would take his hand off her arm. She didn't think he was menacing, like Archie, but she wanted to get away from there. From the dingy shed, the dirty patch of ground, the grey day. The clouds were low and a light drizzle had started. From the port came the mournful bleat of a ship's horn. She shivered.

'Robbie?' Jackie shrugged. 'Not much. Just that he came from Glasgow. The Gorbals, someone said. Whatever that is.'

Isabella had no idea either, but she'd find out. She'd visit the library.

'We could go for a cup of tea,' suggested Jackie, still keeping hold of her arm.

'I've no money,' she said. 'I've lost my job. Goldberg's the tailor's got burned down last night. It was awful.'

'I heard. Jews, aren't they?'

'What if they are?'

'Too many of them round here.'

She pulled her arm away. 'Must go,' she muttered and walked off quickly before he could stop her. Once out of sight she began to run. The world seemed out of kilter, as if it had been knocked off its axis. It had started to tilt the day they'd seen William off at the station, heading for Spain. Heading for the killing fields of Spain. She had heard someone using that phrase on the radio and it had made her blood run cold.

She called in at their local library on her way back. It was full of people, men mostly, reading newspapers and magazines. Out of work. The library was somewhere to go and keep warm. The smell of old clothes and unwashed bodies hit her as she opened the door. A lot of down and outs came in to seek some warmth too.

The librarian on the desk was helpful once Isabella had told her Robbie's story. 'It seems like he might have lived in a part of Glasgow called the Gorbals.'

'The Gorbals?' she repeated. 'Pretty rough area, I seem to have heard. Gangs and that. Razor slashing. Let's see what we can do. The Scots do well for their libraries, so it's said.'

She found the address of the Gorbals' Public Library. 'That might be as good a way as any to track him down. You can try it at least and let me know how you get on.' She wrote it down.

'Thanks,' said Isabella, who doubted if Robbie

would have spent much time in a library but then one never knew. Her dad always said you shouldn't jump to conclusions about people. When she got home she took out a pad of writing paper, her fountain pen and a bottle of blue ink and sat down and began to write a letter to Gorbals' Public Library.

Do you know a boy called Robbie with sandy red hair – she began, then stopped. It looked kind of stupid putting it down like that. There could be dozens of Robbies in Glasgow. Hundreds, even. Thousands. She tore the sheet off the pad, screwed it up, tossed it into the fire and started again.

Her mother looked up from the ironing board and shook her head at the waste of good paper.

'I'm trying to track down Robbie's parents,' said Isabella. If he had any, of course. He might not. He could have grown up in an orphanage.

After another try, Isabella managed to write a letter that more or less satisfied her. She simply set down the facts and on the way to her class that evening she crossed her fingers and popped the envelope into the letter box. She stopped for a moment and stared at the gaping slot. Why should it matter so much to her, to find Robbie's family? She had scarcely known him after all. It was back to William, of course. The long silence from him, with the lack of news, was difficult to bear. It was getting to them all.

Eleven

After her class that evening Isabella asked her teacher if she thought she had reached a high enough standard to look for work as a stenographer by now.

'I do!' said Miss Clarke. 'Why don't you try some of the small businesses? As well as the factories. They all need clerical staff. You won't get anywhere without trying. I'd be delighted to give you a reference,' she added.

Isabella started with Tate and Lyle, the sugar factory in Silvertown, and managed to get inside the door at least. That was a start. She felt nervous sitting in a corridor waiting to hear if she could speak to someone. She tried not to fidget with her gloves. To sit there twisting them in her lap would only show she was nervous. It was one of the tips Miss Clarke had given her. *Try to relax and keep your back straight. No slouching. And look confident, though not overly so.*

Isabella's back was beginning to ache by the time a woman came to summon her. She looked like a telephone operator with twisted plaits parked at either side of her ears.

'Are you the girl looking for work?' The voice was not encouraging. It reminded Isabella of her geometry teacher at school. She nodded.

'Come this way, please.'

The woman strode ahead of Isabella and led her into a small room where another woman sat behind a desk stacked high with files. This one had a bun, a single one, at the back of her head, and she had glasses hanging from her neck on a tape. She raised the glasses to examine Isabella.

'You are looking for a clerical position?' She made it sound as if Isabella was looking for the moon.

'Yes. Miss Clarke has written a reference for me.' Isabella laid it on the desk.

'And who is Miss Clarke, pray?'

'She's my teacher.'

'Night school?'

'Yes.' Would it be better if it were day school?

'I take it you are unemployed?'

'Yes. But just since last night.'

The woman raised an eyebrow.

'I've been working in Goldberg's, you see. It got burned down last night.'

'The tailor's? Oh yes, I think I heard something about that. Did you work there as a seamstress?'

Isabella nodded.

'You have no clerical experience then, I take it?'

'No. Except what I've learned from Miss Clarke.'

'I see.'

For a moment it looked as if that would be the end of that. The woman stared at the wall, stifling a small yawn, then she picked up the envelope that lay between them. She slit it open with a paper knife and withdrew Miss Clarke's beautifully typed letter of recommendation. She read, holding it at arm's length between her long thin fingernails. She too was long and thin and her lips were slightly pursed. She sat back in her chair and looked directly at Isabella. 'Your teacher seems to have a very high opinion of you.'

Not knowing quite how to reply to that Isabella merely nodded. She felt uncomfortable under the woman's penetrating gaze and was finding it difficult not to shift about on the hard chair. Then she thought of her father and how he had always told them not to feel put down by anyone. 'You're as good as the next person,' he'd say.

Isabella lifted her head, squared her shoulders and said, 'I think she does.'

'You're just fourteen, I see.'

'I'll be fifteen soon.'

The woman considered that fact for a moment, then she opened the desk drawer and withdrew a sheaf of paper. 'If you take this form and fill it out I will pass it on to the requisite department. My name is Miss Dawson.'

'Oh, thank you! Thank you very much, Miss Dawson.'

'I wouldn't let your hopes run too high. There are a lot of girls looking for office jobs. We have to turn them away every day.'

Isabella went straight home and sitting down at the kitchen table with a bottle of black ink in front of her – her dad always said black looked more official than blue – she filled her fountain pen and answered the questions. *Name. Address. Date of birth. Education. Work experience.* She took her time, keeping a blotter in place on the line below the one she was working on, making sure she didn't smudge her letters or make ink blots. She only had one chance. One chance!

'You have good writing,' observed her mother, looking over her shoulder. 'Like your papa. He could have been a scholar, if he'd had the chance.'

Isabella blotted the form carefully and when she was sure that each word was completely dry she put on her coat and made her way back to Tate and Lyle's, stopping on the way at a local stationer's shop to buy a large buff-coloured envelope. She slid the form carefully into it and asked if she might borrow a pen and ink for a minute so that she could write 'Miss Dawson' on the front. The stationer was obliging. He knew she had worked at Goldberg's.

'Terrible business, that. There's a few tailors worried sick now in case they get torched and all. Nobody seems to know who done it. You wonder if the police are doing anything about it. Depends how they feel about the Jews, I suppose.'

She didn't want to ask how he felt about them. A lot of people in the East End thought too many had come in, taking their houses and their jobs.

When Isabella reached the sugar factory she asked the man on the door if she could come in to give her letter to Miss Dawson.

'You was here earlier, wasn't you?'

'Yes. She gave me a form to fill in.'

'I'll take it for you.' He held out his hand. 'No need for you to come in.'

Reluctantly she handed it over. 'You won't forget?'

'You can rely on me, miss. Hoping for a job, I suppose? You'll be lucky! They're round here in their droves looking for work. Wasting your time, I tells them.'

Isabella didn't want to hear that again! She left feeling dejected, then told herself to cheer up. He could be exaggerating. He looked the type who liked to pass on bad news. They had more than one in their street like that. When anyone was ill or dying they were at their doors in a flash ready to pass on the bad tidings. Bridie's mum was one of them.

Sean called in at the house for Isabella after tea.

'Coming out?'

'I'll just get my coat.'

'Wrap up warm now,' urged her mother. 'This damp is bad for the bones. No wonder there is much rheumatic in this city. All these fogs!' She shivered. 'Now if we were in Malaga –'

'Just as well we're not,' said Arthur, who was still sitting at the table reading the evening paper. Isabella saw the heading.

SPANISH CIVIL WAR. REPUBLICANS DRIVEN BACK, HEAVY CASUALTIES . . .

'C'mon then,' said Sean, taking Isabella's hand.

It was a cold night with a damp mist creeping up from the river through the buildings, blurring the sodium street lights. The muted sound of foghorns could be heard, giving a warning to seagoing vessels. There was still a hint of burning in the air too, making Isabella shiver. There was nowhere to take shelter. They couldn't afford to sit in a café.

When they reached an alley they took refuge there, putting their backs to the wall. Sean put his arms round Isabella and kissed her. It was the first time that he had. She had been wondering when he would, but Sean was shy compared to some other boys, like the ones living in the shack at the Docks.

'I've been wanting to do that for a while,' he said.

She laughed. 'So have I.'

He cuddled her close to him and they kissed again, breaking apart when a long whistle reached them from the other end of the alley. They could see pinpricks of light up there now. Cigarettes. They smelled them, too. The whistle came again.

'Who's there?' called Sean.

Somebody laughed.

'Is that you, Mickey?' Sean headed up the alleyway at a run.

Isabella followed more slowly. She could just discern the outline of three boys hunkered down in a corner of the lane. Their cigarettes glowed red in the dark.

'What do you think you're doing?' demanded Sean, seizing hold of Mickey by the collar and dragging him up on to his feet. An empty beer bottle rolled across the ground. 'And are you drinkin' and all?'

'Just a fag. What d'you think?' Mickey took a draw on the cigarette and blew smoke into his brother's face.

Sean slapped his face in return, but lightly. 'You know what our ma would do to you? She'd wallop you.'

'She smokes plenty.'

'She buys them, though. Pays for them.'

The other boys decided that it was time for them to go. They slid away into the night.

'You've been thieving again, haven't you?' insisted Sean. 'You'll get nabbed again one of these days, Mickey.

And then you know what'll happen to you.' Mickey had been caught the week before for lifting a poke of toffees from a market stall and got let off with a warning.

All of a sudden a flashlight came sweeping up the alleyway in a wide arc, making them blink.

'Who's that up there?' demanded a voice. The voice of the law.

'Get rid of that stuff, Mickey,' hissed Sean, then he lifted his voice and said, 'It's me, Constable, Sean Flynn. With me girlfriend. Isabella.'

PC MacDade was regularly on their beat. He hailed from the north of Ireland, which he claimed to be a better place than the south. He and Mr Flynn, who was from the south, had almost come to blows over it. Well, not quite, for who was going to take on slugging a copper?

Mickey, as advised, had got rid of the cigarettes by tossing them over the wall and was now crouched down low in its shadow. The light came closer, then stopped.

'I see the two of youse right enough. I'm after some lads. Hallions! They've been in Jolly's nicking fags. Trouble is old Mrs Jolly can't see beyond her nose.'

Lucky for Mickey, thought Isabella.

PC MacDade sighed, exchanged a few more words with Sean and Isabella, emitted a loud yawn and carried on with his rounds.

'You're lucky I didn't turn you in,' said Sean to Mickey once the constable had gone.

'You wouldn't shop me!' retorted Mickey. 'You're my brother.'

'Might be for your own good if I did. Don't let me catch you at it again.' Sean took Mickey by the shoulders and shook him. 'Understand?'

'Cross my heart!'

'All right, get going!' Sean gave his brother a shove. 'And go straight home!'

Mickey fled.

'He's a right divil. You wouldn't know what to do with him so you wouldn't. And our da doesn't bother his head. Since he's not been working he doesn't bother himself about anything except his pigeons.'

Mr Flynn spent his days out in the back yard with his birds and his evenings in the pub. Mrs Flynn hated the pigeons. She pinched her nose when she had to pass them on her way to the lavvy. She said they stank. Their food cost money. She said Mr Flynn cared more about the birds than he did about his children. She was always threatening to strangle the birds. Isabella sometimes wondered if she might not just do it one night when her husband was late coming back from the pub. Sean said he wouldn't put it past her.

They set off home and on their way they met Arthur just as he was alighting from a bus. He was carrying a holdall.

'Where have you been?' asked Isabella.

He shrugged. 'Just out and about.'

She knew he wouldn't give anything away but she could never resist asking. He and Sean started into a conversation about football. Sean supported Tottenham; Arthur, Chelsea. Isabella switched off. They'd be arguing in a minute. Fortunately they didn't have much time for it, they were almost at the Blakes' door.

'See you tomorrow, Issie.' Sean squeezed her arm and carried on home.

Brother and sister went into their house. Their mother looked pleased to see them together.

'We just bumped into each other,' said Isabella quickly. 'Arthur was getting off a bus.'

His mother eyed his bag. 'You weren't playing football in the dark?'

'No, of course not.'

'But you have your sports bag?'

'I went to a gym with a friend.'

'Which friend is that?'

'You wouldn't know him.' Arthur made a move to go upstairs. 'Just a lad I met.'

'Which gym did you go to?' asked his father, lowering the newspaper he'd been reading. 'Poplar?'

'No.' Arthur was uncomfortable. They were waiting for an answer. Isabella too. 'Sort of West End way,' he finally said.

'Oh,' said his mother, 'posh then?'

Arthur didn't answer that one. He went off to bed.

'Do you know this lad, Isabella?' asked her father.

'I might. I think he's called Rupert.'

She too went off to bed, not wanting to say any more. It would only worry her dad if she did.

Twelve

Christmas passed quietly. With William away in Spain fighting in a war, the Blakes had no appetite for celebration. They bought a small tree to stand in the window and laced a few strands of tinsel through its branches, then set a white candle to stand on top. A light for William, said his mother.

Isabella went with her to church in the morning and when they came home they had a good lunch of roasted pork belly with apple sauce and Christmas pudding to follow.

Arthur ate with them, saying barely a word, answering only when spoken to, and as soon as they'd finished their meal he got up, said, 'Thanks for dinner, Mother,' and was off.

'Where *does* he go?' Maria Blake sighed.

Isabella resolved to try and find out. 'Oh, I wish William would write!' she cried, unable to stop herself.

'Don't we all,' said her dad quietly.

A couple of days later her wish was fulfilled. The postman handed in three letters that morning. The men were at work and Isabella was at home with her mother.

'You must be popular,' commented the postman. 'There's one with a foreign stamp. Spanish, I think.'

They recognised William's writing immediately. The envelope was stained and creased. Isabella opened it first, taking care not to rip the envelope too quickly in case she damaged the postcard inside. Her mother watched anxiously.

'What are the stains on it?' cried his mother. 'Blood?'

'Might be mud,' said Isabella uneasily.

'What does it say? Read it to me, Bella, please!'

'*Things have been hot out here* –'

'How does he mean *hot*? It is winter and cold in the north. It is not hot now in Madrid.'

'Perhaps he means that the fighting is hot – you know, fierce – but he probably can't say. I think he'd have to be careful what he writes. He can't give any information away.'

'*Madre Mia*, why did he have to go?' demanded their mother for the umpteenth time.

Isabella often demanded that herself. There were times, lying in bed, when she felt angry with him for going, leaving his family at home worrying themselves sick about him. Even Arthur looked worried when there was a report on the radio about heavy casualties in Spain.

'What else does he say?' asked her mother.

Isabella read on. *'But please do not worry for I am all right. I will give this letter to someone going over the border when I can. I hope you are all well. Much love from William.'*

'What kind of letter is that?' asked his mother. 'He tells us nothing!'

'It lets us know he's alive.'

'When he wrote it!'

That was true. There was no date at the top of the page. Isabella's eyes filled with tears. She put her arms round her mother and they hugged each other.

'We must be brave,' sighed her mother, 'and let Our Lady watch over him.'

The next envelope looked business-like. Isabella opened it with a surge of hope.

'I regret to inform you that we are not currently looking for shorthand typists but we will keep your application on file.' Isabella's spirits dropped as soon as she read the first two words. 'No work for me at Tate and Lyle, Mama, I'm afraid,' she said.

'Never mind, Bella, my love. Someone will want you. You are a clever girl.'

Isabella picked up the remaining letter, which turned out to be from the library in Glasgow. She read it aloud:

'I am sorry to inform you that we have not been able to trace anyone matching the young man Robbie you describe in your letter . . .'

It was perfectly possible, of course, that Robbie had never ever visited the library. Isabella had known that from the start. It might be that he would never be identified. The thought depressed her and her mother too. Robbie might well have to be buried in a pauper's grave, unknown. Now if William were to be found on the battlefield . . . Isabella pulled herself up short. She mustn't let her head run away like that, imagining the worst. But she felt angry with William for going, really angry, for the first time.

'I'm going out, Mama,' she said. 'Do you want anything from the shops?'

Her mother shook her head. 'I will go myself later.' She liked to pick the produce herself and, if necessary, haggle with the stall keeper about the quality and the price.

Isabella did a tour of the shops in the neighbourhood, omitting the butcher, the fishmonger and the pawnshop. Apart from not fancying working in any of them, none of the shopkeepers could afford to pay for help.

'Sorry, love. The wife helps out from time to time. I don't have to pay nothin' to her.'

Or if it wasn't the wife, it would be a daughter, or some other relative. They did the cleaning too. That was the story in most shops these days.

Isabella went further afield, towards the City. She considered trying Oxford Street and some of the big stores there. 'Why not?' her father would say if he'd been there.

'Why not?' she said to herself, but as soon she was inside one of those grand emporiums her courage failed her. How could she possibly ask if there were any jobs going? But she lingered. After the chill of the street the warmth of the store wrapped itself round her. She caught a whiff of perfume in the air. Jewellery glittered on the counters. She wandered round in a daze. Everything was so new and so expensive! She looked down at her coat. It wasn't shabby but it was made of cheap material compared to the ones for sale here.

An assistant dressed in a neat black dress was staring at her. 'Can I help you?' The voice was icy, disdainful, not encouraging, though Isabella thought that maybe she was imagining it.

'Well,' she began, but the assistant had turned her attention to a woman in a fur coat. Her voice was now as sweet as golden syrup. Isabella could scarcely blame her. She would want to make a sale. She would have to make a sale or else she might lose her job.

Isabella wandered round the racks of clothes. Another assistant was eyeing her now. She had craned her neck to keep Isabella in her line of vision. Perhaps she thought Isabella was looking for an opportunity to nick something.

Isabella left and headed towards a street where the shops were not quite so expensive. She stopped at a shoe shop and gazed in at the window. There were pretty shoes for sale but there appeared to be no customers. An assistant, a girl who looked not much older than Isabella herself, yawned. She saw Isabella looking in at her and smiled sheepishly. Isabella went inside. The girl looked pleased. She became wide awake at the sight of a possible customer.

'Can I help you?' she asked in a bright voice.

'I was just wondering if there might be a vacancy.'

'A vacancy?' The girl's smile faded.

'I don't suppose there is,' said Isabella hurriedly.

They chatted for a moment about jobs, or the lack of them, and the girl complained about being in there all day long and how boring it was. She wanted to be a mannequin.

Isabella moved on. She didn't feel like going home. She went back to Oxford Street and cut across Hyde Park. The sun had come out. She kept walking southwards, towards the river. She was in Sloane Street now, in Chelsea. Had she meant to come this way, or had it just happened? What did she think she would find out by coming here?

A workman, a house painter in white overalls, was leaning against a lamppost smoking a cigarette, taking a break. She approached him.

'Excuse me,' she said, 'but I wonder if you could tell me

if there is a gymnasium round here? A friend mentioned something . . .'

'A gymnasium?' The man frowned. 'Not as I can think of.'

It didn't look like the kind of area where you would find a sports building.

'Thanks, anyway,' said Isabella, ready to move on.

'Hey, wait a minute! There's the Fascists' building.'

Isabella stopped dead in her tracks and turned back to him.

'They've got their headquarters in Kings Road, next to the Duke of York's army barracks. Used to be a teachers' training college, so I 'eard. Big place it is. We calls it the Black House, 'cause they dress in black for the most part. Black or grey trousers, black tunic tops, black peaked caps, black boots. Rum lot they are. Friends of Hitler. They'd be locked up if I had my way.'

'Would they have a gymnasium?'

'I'd imagine so. They're dead keen on fitness. Seems they've got everything in there. Parade grounds, dining hall, mess rooms, offices, dormitories. Pal of mine did some work for them one time. Said they were like an army. Couple of hundred of them, maybe more. They live in. They're out and about all the time though, giving out leaflets, recruiting, trying to get young lads to join them. They take on women, too. You don't want to go near them, luv.'

'My friend must have been thinking of somewhere else.'

'Think he must.' The painter tossed the butt of his cigarette into the gutter. 'Better get back to the grind before the boss comes round.'

They parted and Isabella walked on towards the Kings Road.

She found the building easily. It was big and rather ugly.

'Hello there! Come to join us?'

She whirled round. There stood Rupert, spruce in his uniform, booted and capped. He looked handsome, there was no denying that.

'Have you?' he asked.

'Certainly not!' she retorted, feeling her cheeks heating up. She half turned, ready to go.

'Hey, just a minute! Don't fly off like that! You've got the wrong idea about us. Everybody does.'

She hesitated.

'We're not against the Jews. Our leader forbids anti-Semitism.' Rupert came closer to her. 'Why don't you let me buy you a cup of tea, Isabella, and I'll tell you what we do stand for?'

She hesitated and he took her arm.

Thirteen

Isabella found herself facing Rupert across a café table. She couldn't understand how she had got here. She'd followed him as if in a dream. Why had she agreed to come? He was looking straight at her, engaging her with his eyes, which were an intense, very clear blue. His gaze was compelling, hypnotic almost. He was quite different from any other person she had met. And he was handsome, she had to acknowledge that. She glanced away from him, picked up her cup and drank a few sips of tepid tea, aware all the time that his eyes were still on her. She had to concentrate so as not to spill any tea in the saucer.

'Has your tea gone cold? Here, let me top it up for you.' He lifted the teapot and filled her cup.

It was the kind of café that served tea in silver teapots with fine bone-china cups and saucers decorated with pink roses. There was not a mug in sight. The waitresses wore black dresses with white frilly aprons and caps and were very polite. Isabella had never been in such a café before. Everything must be expensive too. It was a far cry from the places she and Sean frequented! She put Sean out of her mind. He'd go raving mad if he were to walk in and see her sitting there, drinking tea with a Blackshirt. But there was no likelihood of him doing that.

Their waitress approached them now. 'Everything all right, sir?'

'We'd like a fresh pot, if you please, Mary. You may take this lot away.' Rupert swept his hand across the table without disturbing anything on it. 'And bring us a selection of your cream cakes. My friend might like a chocolate éclair. Would you, Isabella?'

She had no time to reply for Mary had already gone to fetch a tray and within seconds was back to clear the used dishes from their table. Her task completed, she glided off back through the swing doors into the nether regions of the café, leaving Isabella to face Rupert again. She wanted to tell him that she must go home, that her mother would be expecting her, but somehow it seemed too difficult. She felt uneasy, was trying not to shift about on her seat. Rupert had called her his friend yet she hardly knew him.

'Relax!' he said.

She blushed.

'Now tell me,' he continued, leaning forward across the table, 'what is your interest in us?'

She hesitated. 'You mean the Fascists . . .' she began awkwardly.

'The British Union of Fascists, yes. We are a perfectly legal party, you know. You have no need to be embarrassed.'

She felt even more so now. She wanted to get up and go but somehow she couldn't make a move and here came the waitress advancing towards them, carrying a tray laden with fresh cups and saucers and plates and a teapot and a large plate of cream cakes.

'Shall I serve, sir?'

'If you please.'

The waitress spread a linen napkin across Isabella's lap. She asked what Isabella took in her tea.

'Milk, please, no sugar.'

'Excellent,' declared Rupert. 'It is good that you don't take sugar. It is bad for the teeth and pollutes the system.'

Isabella wished now that she had asked for four lumps.

'One must look after one's health,' Rupert continued. 'Fitness is important, don't you agree?'

She nodded.

'Exercise, posture, diet . . . all are vital if we want to develop a healthy, upstanding race, but sadly too many people don't adhere to that. Look at the round shoulders you see in the streets, the bent backs, the bow legs!' Rupert spoke as if he were delivering a lecture. Perhaps this was part of the speech that he gave in that hall in Poplar.

Isabella would have liked to retaliate, to tell him that people, especially in the East End, didn't have much choice. They couldn't afford good food and some of them lived in damp houses with no running hot water and privies in the back yard. The Blakes had an outside privy themselves, after all.

'And sadly they often drink too much,' added Rupert.

Isabella thought of Mr Flynn rolling back from the pub every night. She nodded.

'Do you do any sport yourself, Isabella?'

'I like swimming.'

Rupert nodded his approval. 'We have an excellent pool and gymnasium in our headquarters should you care to sample it?'

'I don't know . . .'

'You would enjoy the pool. I'll arrange it.'

'Cake, miss?' The waitress had been standing patiently beside their table holding out the plate.

'Take the chocolate éclair,' instructed Rupert.

Isabella lifted her head. 'But it's got sugar in it!'

'On special occasions one is allowed to indulge oneself.'

Special occasions? Was that what he thought this was?

'Give my friend an éclair, if you please. The largest one.' Rupert pointed to it.

The waitress transferred the éclair on to Isabella's plate with a pair of tongs. Isabella stared at the fat brown sausage bulging with cream and felt sick. Normally she would have dived straight into an éclair. And enjoyed it.

'Aren't you going to eat it, Isabella?' asked Rupert.

'Oh yes . . . yes, of course.' She lifted the dainty little knife and fork sitting at either side of the plate, cut off a piece of the éclair and put it into her mouth. She was conscious of Rupert watching her all the time. He had waved the waitress away when she had offered him a cake, saying that he never ate sweet things. They were bad for the teeth. He had very white, strong-looking teeth. *All the better to eat you up with.*

Isabella struggled with her pastry. Why didn't she just get up and go! She couldn't understand herself. She didn't look up. She didn't want to meet his eyes.

'Is it good?' he asked.

'Yes, thank you.'

She didn't think it was all that good. It was a bit too sweet for her taste, and gloppy with it, and for a moment she thought she might gag but she forced herself to eat every bit. She parked the knife and fork neatly, side by side, on the clean plate.

'Bravo!' declared Rupert. 'For a minute I thought you weren't going to make it. But I have the feeling that you are a determined young lady and don't give up easily. Am I right?'

'I must be going,' Isabella said, reaching down for her bag, which she had put on the floor.

'Oh, come, don't go yet! We haven't had much time to talk. To get to know each other. You wanted to know more about our organisation, didn't you? Well, just let me say that our aim first and foremost is to protect our country. To make it strong. What can you have to say against that?'

'Who are you protecting it from?' She felt herself firming up. She lifted her head and looked him in the eye. 'Adolf Hitler?'

'Nonsense!' He laughed. 'Hitler is not our enemy.'

'My dad says different.'

'What can he know? Don't misunderstand me. I'm sure he is a fine man but he's not educated, is he?'

'Did Arthur tell you that?' asked Isabella angrily. Wait till she got her hands on him! 'My father went to school and he's gone regularly to night classes and educated himself. He's read most of Charles Dickens's novels.'

'Excellent!'

'Yes, it is excellent!' Isabella was aware that she was talking loudly. She had never had such an argument in a public place before. She went on, 'I am proud of my dad.'

'I'm pleased to know that. One should respect one's elders. I have no quarrel with that unless, of course, they have taken false paths. You see, we might have more in common than you think.'

Isabella doubted that. She continued, 'My dad knows

about the world. He reads newspapers and he listens to the wireless.'

'You can't believe everything you hear on the BBC, you know. They are biased, I am sorry to say.'

'About Fascists?'

He nodded. 'Though many eminent people support us. Titled people. You want to improve our nation, don't you?'

'Well, yes . . .'

'We want to educate young people and teach them how to keep fit. Anything wrong in that?'

'No . . .'

'Trouble is that we have too many people coming in to our communities without qualifications or money to sustain themselves. Look at all the Irish there are in the East End! Most of them don't work.'

'Nor can a lot of people in the East End! There are no jobs.'

'Exactly. We need to do something about that.'

They were attracting attention. Heads were turned. Customers had stopped eating. Some looked amused.

Isabella pushed back her chair and sprang quickly up on to her feet. 'Thank you for the tea and cake.'

'Wait! I'll walk you to your bus stop.'

'I don't need to be walked, thank you!'

Rupert was clicking his fingers in the air and signalling to the waitress. 'Bill, please!' he shouted.

Isabella escaped and once outside she ran, dodging round pedestrians as she went. She was a fast runner, had always come first in the girls' races at school. When she reached a stop a bus came immediately. She didn't even wait to see where it was going. She just leaped aboard and the bus pulled out from the kerb. He wouldn't catch up with her now.

But she had a feeling she would see him again.

Fourteen

She was to see Rupert the following Saturday evening. She and her mother had been engaged to perform their flamenco act in the Queen's Theatre in Poplar again. As they came on to the stage to a wave of applause her eyes swept over the audience and the first person they lighted on was Rupert standing at the back. She hesitated for a moment and her mother gave her a quick sideways look. The lights dimmed, the audience vanished and Isabella, caught up in the music and the dance, forgot about him.

At the end, after taking their bows, she looked out into the audience again and her eyes were drawn to him unwittingly. She didn't want to look at him and yet here she was doing just that. He was still standing, his hands raised high above his head, clapping slowly. She could tell he was smiling, even from that distance. She glanced quickly away and searched for Sean and there he was, in the middle of a row, on his feet, cheering, alongside her father and Bridie.

'*Encore! Encore!*'

Her dad was waiting outside the stage door afterwards with Bridie and Sean. He hugged them and said they had been fantastic. They started to walk, Maria and Jim Blake going ahead of the young people. Behind them, Isabella walked in the middle between Bridie and Sean, her arms linked with theirs.

'That Rupert was in the audience,' said Bridie. 'He couldn't take his eyes off you. Think he fancies you. Sean doesn't like that, do you, Sean?'

Sean glowered at his sister. 'He'd better not come near me, that's all. Bloody Fascist.'

'He and his chums were giving out leaflets before the show, same as before,' said Bridie in a low voice. 'I told a girl who'd taken one to have nothing to do with it. I told her they were a bad lot. He heard me. I could tell he wasn't pleased. I don't know how you managed to have tea with him, Issie, without throwing up.'

Sean turned to Isabella. 'You were drinkin' tea with him?' he asked incredulously. 'Where was that?'

'In a café in Chelsea.'

'In a café in *Chelsea*?"

'I didn't want to.'

'How'd you mean? You didn't want to? Did he drag you there?'

'No. Course not.'

'What were you doin' there then?' Sean was getting worked up.

'Looking for Arthur,' said Isabella. 'Oh, leave it, Sean!'

Her parents looked back at them, disturbed by their raised voices.

'We're going for a bus,' called her father. 'What about you young 'uns?

'Shall we walk?' suggested Isabella.

The other two agreed. It was a nice night, and for once there was no fog. None of them felt like going inside yet. The streets were full of people.

'Don't be too late now, Isabella,' cautioned her dad, who didn't mind her being out as long as she was with Sean.

'I won't be, Dad,' she promised.

They parted and the three young ones sauntered on down the street. There were still some street performers going, a juggler, a tap dancer, and even a couple of girls trying to do flamenco!

'*Olé!*' called out Isabella.

The girls giggled and one of them shouted '*Olé!*' in return.

Sean asked no more questions about Rupert.

Isabella was in a good mood. Their act had gone down well. She had enjoyed her dancing, and so had the audience. It had given her a warm glow inside. And here she was strolling along the street, her hands tucked into the arms of her two closest friends. But when she saw Rupert up ahead with two other boys her mood changed abruptly.

He had seen her too. He was standing on the pavement, feet astride, hands in his pockets. He might have been smiling, she was not sure. Isabella tightened her grip on Sean's arm.

As they drew closer Bridie recognised him. 'There's that nut case,' she said in a loud voice. 'The idiot who thinks Hitler's the bees' knees.'

Rupert made no move to stand aside when they reached him. He looked at Bridie.

'You should watch what you say, miss,' he said softly. 'Blackening my name like that, and out in the street too. It could get you into trouble.'

'Don't you dare threaten my sister!' Sean's temper was rising. He pushed the girls aside and stepped forward to confront Rupert.

'Come back, Sean!' cried Isabella, catching him by the sleeve, but he shrugged her off.

Sean stepped forward. In seconds the two men had squared up to each other, ignoring the girls' pleas.

Sean landed the first blow but it only glanced off Rupert's shoulder as he ducked. Then Rupert's right arm came up and out in a wide sweep and made contact with Sean's chin. Sean was no weakling but Rupert, it was obvious, was a well-trained and experienced boxer.

Sean went down with a whack on to the pavement where he lay flat on his back, winded.

'Sean!' cried Bridie, collapsing beside him.

'I'm all right,' he muttered, struggling to get up. He pushed Bridie away. He didn't want his sister to be seen coming to help him. He staggered as he found his feet again.

Isabella was left facing Rupert, who stood there smiling.

'Your friend should be more careful about whom he takes on,' he said.

Sean was starting to lunge in his direction.

'Leave it, Sean!' cried Isabella, and to Rupert, 'Go away and leave us alone! Your lot don't belong here.'

'Some of us do,' said Rupert, speaking in a calm, quiet voice. The brush with Sean had not roused him. 'What about brother Arthur?' he asked.

'Stay away from my brother! You've brainwashed him.'

'Brainwashed him? Do you really think so? Are his brains that easily washed?'

Isabella was tempted to have a go and wallop Rupert herself but she decided that would only amuse him. She looked around. They had to get out of here as fast as they could. Apart from Rupert himself there were his two heavy-looking mates.

Bridie was clinging on to her brother, holding him

back. She might be thin and not too tall but she was determined when her temper was up. As it was now.

'We're going home, Sean!' said Isabella. 'We want nothing more to do with this lot!'

'Eejits!' screamed Bridie.

'Eejits, are we?' said Rupert. 'We'll see about that.' He made a move towards them and eased Bridie out of the way.

She staggered but rallied to scream at the top of her voice. 'Scum!' she cried in his face.

'Scum, am I?' Rupert sounded amused. But there was steel in his voice now.

His two mates, who, until now, had been standing idly by looking bored, came to life, ready to join in any fray that might develop.

'What's goin' on here?' thundered a voice behind them. For once Isabella was glad to see a couple of bobbies descending on them, twirling their batons.

'Nothing, Constable,' said Rupert smoothly. 'Only a little private argument. We were just about to be on our way.'

'Best go then!'

'Come on, lads,' said Rupert. He looked back. 'I'll be seeing you, Isabella.'

'Don't you dare come near her!' Sean was ready to launch himself at Rupert again when one of the policemen put a restraining hand on his arm.

Rupert didn't even turn round. He sauntered off down the street with his two pals.

The constable watched them go. 'What are you kids doin' hanging out with that bunch? D'you not know they're Blackshirts? Mosley men? They hold meetings, recruiting anyone who's stupid enough to be taken in by them.'

'Why don't you stop them?' asked Isabella.

'They're not illegal. Now, if we was to go to war with Hitler, that would change –'

'We won't though, will we?' cried Bridie. 'Go to war?'

'Hope not. We're not wantin' any more wars. I lost my big brother in the Battle of the Somme. That's what makes me want to kick that lot when I see them.' The constable pointed his baton up the street in the direction the three men had taken.

'Don't blame you,' said Sean.

They all knew about the battlefields of the Somme, the place in France where thousands of young men had died in the Great War.

'Best steer clear of Mosleyites,' warned the constable as a parting shot.

But how did you steer clear of your own brother when he lived in the same house? Isabella hadn't told her friends about Arthur being involved in the Blackshirts. She couldn't always rely on Bridie to keep her mouth shut and she didn't want it to be known up and down the street. Her parents didn't seem to suspect what he was up to, not as far as she could tell.

Arthur was in his room when Isabella arrived home. She tapped on the door and put her head round it. He was lying on his bed reading a magazine. She went in.

'What do you want?' he asked sharply.

'Arthur,' she said, closing the door behind her, 'you should be careful about the company you keep.'

He sat upright. 'What are you talking about?'

'Your friend Rupert's a bad influence.'

'That's rubbish! Just because he admires Hitler. Well, so do I,' added Arthur defiantly. 'I don't see why we should let all these useless people come into our country.'

'Which people are you thinking of?'

'You know! The Lithuanians. The Jews. The Irish. They're everywhere.'

'Is that right?' demanded Isabella, her temper rising.

'Half of them don't even work.'

'Maybe they can't get any,' Isabella shouted at him.

'They're lazy. Look at your friends the Flynns!'

'Sean has a job and the others work when they can get it.'

'We want people who pull their weight. Who can help to make our country greater.' Arthur was getting steamed up too. He might as well have been standing on a platform. 'We want to keep Britain for the British!'

'What about Mama? Would you put her out? She's not British.'

'She's as good as. She's married to Dad.'

'She's Spanish to the core,' returned Isabella. She couldn't carry on with this stupid conversation any longer. She went out and slammed the door behind her.

She met her father on the stairs.

'What's going on?' he asked. 'Sounded like you and Arthur were having a bit of a barney?'

Isabella shrugged.

Her father looked thoughtful but let her pass him and go on down the stairs.

Fifteen

'There's a letter for you, Isabella,' her mother called to her up the stairs.

The postman had just been. Isabella had heard him chatting with her mother, complaining about the weather. A fog was wreathing the city yet again, obscuring the rooftops. The sound of foghorns floated up from the river, making her feel cooped up and restless. She was in the middle of cleaning her parents' bedroom and changing the sheets.

Her mother was telling the postman that in Spain they didn't have these terrible cold wet fogs.

'Sunshine all year round, eh?'

'Almost.'

'But you wouldn't want to be in Spain at present, would you? It's terrible, what's going on there. All that fighting! Young men getting killed. Our young men. Don't know why they have to go, mind you . . . Oh, I'm sorry, Mrs Blake. I was forgetting about your William.

He's all right, I take it?'

'As far as we know.'

As far as we know. It had become a kind of ritual, giving this answer to everyone who asked. The trouble was they knew virtually nothing. It was as if William had dropped into a great black hole.

'A letter, Isabella,' her mother repeated.

Isabella leaned over the banisters. 'For me?'

'It looks as if it's from an office,' added her mother. 'Your name is typed - Miss Isabella Blake.'

Isabella ran quickly down the stairs and took the envelope from her mother's hand. She ripped it open and pulled out a crisp sheet of white paper.

'It's from Tate and Lyle! They want me to come for an interview! Tomorrow. Isn't that wonderful, Mama? I might soon have a job.'

They hugged each other. Isabella had begun to believe that she'd never even get an interview.

'You must borrow my new red coat,' insisted her mother. 'Your blue one needs to go to cleaners. And my brown leather gloves and my Sunday handbag. They are such good Spanish leather. You must look smart! And what about a hat?'

'No, Mama, no hat!'

Isabella went to her interview dressed in her mother's coat and carrying the good handbag. She was not sure about the handbag, it was on the large side, but her mother would have been offended had she not taken it. Anyway, Isabella reasoned, the size of your handbag would scarcely matter.

The woman who interviewed her was very pleasant. She smiled and invited Isabella to take a seat and at the end thanked her for coming and said she would let her know. Isabella felt she had done well, she had answered every question and the woman had nodded as if in approval.

'We will be in touch soon,' she told Isabella.

On her way out Isabella saw another girl sitting in the outer room chewing her nails. And as she walked along the corridor she passed yet another heading for the waiting room. This one was tall and wore a royal blue coat and hat to match with a long blue feather. She carried herself with an air of assurance, her head held high.

Isabella returned home feeling a little subdued. It was silly of her not to have realised that there would be competition for the job. She should have expected it.

'I don't think the hat will get the other girl the job,' said Isabella's father dryly when she told him she thought she had no chance and that the other girl had looked very confident.

'Maybe too confident?' suggested her father.

The following morning there was no post, or the next.

'You can't expect to hear so quickly,' said her father.

'But the lady who interviewed me said *soon*. And a letter posted one day normally arrives the next, doesn't it, if it's within the city boundary?'

'I believe so. But the woman might have had to think about it.'

On the third day Isabella went out into the hall and stood on the front doorstep. It gave her a better view of the street. Her dad had left for work, as had Arthur. He'd gone out very early as usual. They hardly seemed to see him these days and when he was at home he had little to say.

'Close the door please, Isabella,' called her mother, who was on her knees stoking up the fire. 'You are letting the heat out.'

Isabella closed the door and stood by the window in the living room. When she saw the postman pass the window she jumped up and went back to the door. He was not their usual postman.

'Where's Ernie?' she cried after him.

The postman looked round. 'He got took ill in the night with his stummick.'

'Any post?'

The postman shook his head.

Isabella couldn't help feeling dejected, even though her mother kept telling her it was too soon to give up hope. The trouble was that she hated having nothing to do. She was restless. Sean was at the yard and even

Bridie had work at present. She was waiting on tables in a café further into town. Isabella hadn't exactly enjoyed working in the tailor's but it was better than being out of work. Mr Goldberg was trying to pick up the pieces of his business, starting again in his own house, doing the machining himself while his wife did the buttonholes and other finicky jobs. The money he was making would scarcely be enough to stay alive on but it was better than nothing. The fire raisers had never been caught of course.

'You can go shopping for me,' said Isabella's mother, finally. 'We're needing bread and, yes, potatoes and carrots. Save me carrying those heavy things.'

On her way along to the shops Isabella heard someone shouting behind her. She turned. One of the neighbours was standing at her door waving an envelope. Isabella ran back.

'I think this is for you, love,' said the woman. 'You're Jim Blake's girl, aren't you? Postman put this in my door by mistake.'

Isabella ripped the envelope open on the spot.

The letter was brief, but gave her the news she so desperately wanted. 'I've got the job!' she shouted.

'Aren't you the lucky one?' said the woman.

That evening Isabella delved into her savings and took Bridie and Sean to the pictures downtown to celebrate. They saw Charlie Chaplin in *Modern Times*.

They were still laughing about it when they came surging out in the midst of the crowd until Isabella caught sight of Rupert standing on the pavement with Arthur. Rupert seemed to be everywhere! Not that he could have been following them but, nevertheless, Isabella felt riled and her laughter died. So did Sean's. Isabella felt his arm tense over hers.

'I'll get him one of these days,' he muttered.

'Don't,' said Isabella. 'He's not worth it.'

Both Arthur and Rupert had seen them. Arthur looked embarrassed, as if he would prefer to avoid them, which he no doubt would, but Rupert had taken up a position that meant they would have to pass him. He was standing his ground and there was no room for manoeuvre as the cinema audience milled around.

When they drew level with him he said, 'Good evening, Miss Isabella. Did you enjoy the picture?'

'Yes, thank you,' said Isabella. She eyed Arthur but he was looking away from them, in the other direction.

They pushed on, the three of them, with Rupert keeping level. Arthur trailed behind. Isabella felt furious with him. Had Rupert quizzed him? Surely he hadn't told Rupert where she was going that evening? Arthur had changed so much since he'd become involved with the Blackshirts.

The crowd began to thin out with people trailing off in different directions.

'He's a great actor, isn't he, Chaplin?' said Rupert.

Isabella nodded. She could feel Sean boiling up next to her, spoiling for a fight.

'Of course he is quite unique,' continued Rupert. 'He has a very small underdeveloped body.'

No good for the Blackshirts then, thought Isabella.

But Sean's temper snapped. He pushed the girls aside and whirled round to confront Rupert. Sean would never be one to stand back from a fight. His mother despaired of her sons, so she said, though Isabella thought a part of her enjoyed their reputation. The Fighting Flynns! Sean was the son who stirred up the least trouble. But he was facing Rupert now.

'Why don't you get lost?' he demanded.

'It's a free world,' returned Rupert in an amused voice. 'In moderation of course, but everyone is entitled to walk along the street if they so wish.'

Sean lunged forward and Rupert neatly sidestepped. Several people had stopped to watch.

'Leave it, Sean!' cried Isabella. He already felt humiliated from their previous encounter, she knew that. They had to get him away from here as fast as possible.

Rupert was laughing. Looking around, Isabella realised that Arthur had disappeared into the night.

'Come on, Sean,' she said firmly. 'We're going home.'

Sean struggled against the girls and tried to push them aside. Rupert watched them, standing a few feet away with a smile on his face. The situation was saved, once again, by the arrival of the police, two in number, lazily swinging their batons, out to patrol Saturday night hotspots.

'All right, break it up!' ordered one of them. 'You're blocking the pavement.'

'I'll say goodnight then, Isabella,' said Rupert, giving her a small bow. 'I'll see you soon.' He walked away, as if he hadn't a care in the world.

'Stay away from me,' she said in a low voice.

'Bothering you, was he?' asked the second constable. 'He's very well spoken, I must say. Very courteous always. We often see him around, don't we, Harold? Nicely dressed too.'

'He's a Blackshirt,' said Sean.

The policeman nodded. 'I'm not for them but, mind you, there's something to be said for some of their ideas.'

'Such as?' asked Isabella.

'Britain for the British, of course.'

Sean looked ready to rise to that until Bridie took him by the arm. 'Come on,' she said, 'we're going home! *Now!*'

Sixteen

Sean couldn't get Rupert out of his mind. He kept going on about him, talking about what he would do to him, smash his face in for a start. He was going to join a boxing club and get some proper training.

'What good d'you think it'd do you, if you smashed his face in?' asked his sister. 'He'd only come back after you.'

'You'd start a war,' said Isabella.

'So what?' retorted Sean. 'Sometimes you have to. Look at your William, out there in Spain.'

'He didn't start it,' Isabella said wearily. She didn't want to talk about Will. She turned to Bridie, 'Come on, let's you and I go for a walk! Let's get away from here.'

'Good idea.'

Isabella ran off to let her parents know not to expect her for supper. Then she and Bridie linked arms and set off downtown. The day was bright, if cold. They walked briskly, humming under their breath. There were a lot of people about, it being Saturday afternoon. Most workers finished at lunchtime on a Saturday.

'He's an eejit, our Sean, at times,' said Bridie. 'Not as bad as the rest of our lot, though.' She sighed. 'Those lads are always in trouble. And as for Mickey! He'd like to imagine he's some kind of daredevil like Errol Flynn in *Captain Blood*.'

'Doesn't mean Errol's a daredevil running about with a sword in his hand in real life. He could be as meek as mild. I heard he wasn't all that tall and had to stand on a box for some scenes.' Both girls laughed at the idea.

'Tell that to Mickey! Errol's his hero. Dear knows how that boy will end up.' Bridie sighed and changed the subject. 'Oh, I wish William would come home!'

So did Isabella.

Bridie told Isabella she prayed for William every night. So did Isabella, but she sometimes thought she was talking into a dark hole.

'We must have faith,' her mother would say. She went to church every morning to pray for her son.

There had been no news from William for a while. The only information they could get was from the wireless or newspapers but none of that was of much help since they didn't even know where exactly in Spain William was. They had heard only that lunchtime that there had been a fierce battle involving British battalions of the

International Brigade at a place called Jarama not far from Madrid. Franco's army had had tanks and aircraft cover, unlike the Republicans, who'd been left cowering on the ground with no planes to protect them. Casualties had been high. The news had been a bit confused but it seemed there had been many casualties. Isabella had had a terrible sense of foreboding listening to the report. She had been unable to finish her meal.

'Turn that thing off, Jim!' her mother had said to her father.

He had turned the wireless off leaving a feeling of emptiness in the room once the sound had gone. Isabella had been glad to get out into the fresh air.

The weather turned colder as the two friends made their way home much later that evening. There was rain in the wind. Not many people were abroad. As they drew level with their local pub the door swung open to let two or three customers out. The clock had just struck ten, closing time.

'Time gentlemen, please!' they heard the barman call. 'All out, if you will! Come on now, let's be having you!'

Nobody seemed to be moving. There'd be a bouncer on hand to pitch out the drunks. Before the door swung shut the girls caught a fleeting glimpse of Bridie's dad, seated at the bar, his cap perched on the back of his head, an empty pint glass in his hand, roaring drunk.

'He'll be smashing the place up when he comes home,' Bridie said bitterly. 'He goes for me mum, you know,' she added.

Isabella squeezed her friend's arm. It was the only thing she could do for there wasn't much she could say. It was common knowledge that Paddy Flynn knocked his wife about if his sons weren't home. When they were, they stopped him.

'You're lucky,' said Bridie.

'I know,' said Isabella.

'You're dad's a gent.'

'Yes.'

'William takes after him, don't you think?'

'I do.'

They parted at Bridie's door and agreed to meet the next day.

Please, God, thought Isabella as she pushed open her front door, *bring William back to us*.

Isabella was due to start work at Tate and Lyle's the day after her fifteenth birthday. Her mother made a chocolate cake and invited Bridie and Sean to join them for tea. Sean gave Isabella a blue glass necklace and Bridie gave her an embroidered handkerchief. From her parents she got a book, *Wuthering Heights* by Emily Brontë. Arthur, when he came in later, tossed a box of Cadbury's milk chocolates on to the table in front of her.

She went to bed happy with the thought that she would be starting work next day. It would be a relief to have a job to go to in the mornings and to join the throng of workers weaving through the streets. It would be a relief too to have something else to think about other than William.

She soon made friends with the girl she worked beside. Madge was older than Isabella by a year or more, and she also lived in the East End. She was pretty with wavy blonde hair and she wore a perky little emerald green hat to work. She insisted that you got on better in life if you wore a hat. Isabella hated hats. She liked the feeling of her long black hair blowing free in the wind, especially after spending long hours huddled over a typewriter. Madge said she should get her hair bobbed, it was more modern. Isabella couldn't imagine being without her long hair. In spite of their differences she and Madge got on well and they walked part of the way home together.

On the third day when they came out of the factory *he* was there, dressed in a black trench coat tightly belted at the waist, waiting, watching, on the opposite side of the road. Isabella shrank back.

'What's the matter?' asked Madge.

'You see him over there?'

'Good-looker. Well dressed, too. A real smasher. What's wrong with him?'

Isabella shrugged. She didn't want to say too much. 'He bothers me.'

'I wouldn't mind if someone like that was botherin' me.'

Rupert crossed the road to join them and Madge flashed him a smile.

'Aren't you going to introduce us, Isabella?' he asked.

'Me name's Madge,' she said, introducing herself.

'And I'm Rupert.' He extended his hand and Madge took it.

'Pleased to meet you, I'm sure, Rupert,' she said.

'The pleasure is all mine, Madge,' he returned in his smooth, even voice.

Isabella was doing all she could to control her anger. How did he know where she worked? There could only be one answer to that. Wait till she saw Arthur! He was lying low these days, leaving the table after meals as quickly as he could, going out immediately afterwards, not saying where he was going, coming in late when everyone was in bed, creeping up the stairs carefully, avoiding the one that creaked.

Rupert fell into step beside them, and soon he and Madge began to chat about pictures they'd seen and actors and actresses they liked. Madge loved Shirley Temple and Deanna Durbin. And she thought Clark Gable was the most handsome man she'd ever seen!

'In the pictures, that is,' she added, giving Rupert a coy look.

He returned it with a smile.

Isabella didn't believe that he was in the least bit interested in discussing film stars. He was just worming his way in, turning on the charm, softening up his next victim. Before they'd gone much further he was telling Madge about a talk he was giving that evening. She was impressed.

'A talk about society today? My, you must be a clever one! Mustn't he, Issie?'

He produced a leaflet from his pocket. He probably carried them with him wherever he went, thought Isabella. Just in case.

'Come along if you feel like it, Madge,' Rupert said. 'You'd be most welcome. It's free entry.'

'I might just do that. I've nothing else going, not tonight. What about you, Issie?'

Isabella shook her head. 'I must be getting home. See you tomorrow, Madge.'

With that she turned abruptly and set off at a rapid pace. She didn't feel she was running out on Madge. Madge would be delighted to be left alone with Rupert. But Isabella noticed that he had looked less pleased.

Isabella walked home briskly, her head boiling up furiously at the thought of her brother telling Rupert where she was working. Arthur knew she didn't want anything to do with him and she was sure, too, that he wouldn't want her to be involved in Rupert's activities. It seemed as if Rupert ruled. Whatever he wanted he got.

She saw Bridie up the street and waved, calling out, 'See you after tea.'

The Blakes' house was never locked except at night, once everybody was in. Isabella pushed open the living-room door. Her parents were there and, lying on the sofa, was a young man, which made her heart stop for a moment. It reminded her of when Robbie had turned up out of the blue. The bandage round this boy's head was stained with blood, old dried blood, just as Robbie's had been. Then she realised that something else was wrong. The splint on his right hand looked odd. Four of his fingers appeared to be missing, leaving only his thumb. She almost cried out but stopped herself in time, clasping her hand over her mouth.

'This is Angus,' said her dad, who was crouched down beside the visitor. 'He fought in the Battle of Jarama alongside William.'

Seventeen

Isabella's stomach lurched and she thought she was going to be sick.

'Sit down, love,' said her mother, pulling forward a chair for her. 'You have gone quite pale.'

'William?' stammered Isabella. 'Is he –?'

'We don't know,' said her father. 'Angus lost sight of him during the battle.' He stood up and for a moment looked as if he were staring into the far distance, perhaps to this place called Jarama. What did he see there? William lying dead on the battlefield? Isabella felt a ripple of fear run through her body like an electric shock. Her dad went back to sit in his chair, a big old brown leather one that had belonged to his father. He sighed.

Isabella turned to Angus. 'How did you know where to find us?'

'William gave me your address. In case we got separated during the fighting. Said if I ever needed a place to stay in London . . . He put it on a piece of paper. I have it here in my pocket.' Angus spoke slowly, wheezing with every word. 'It was terrible. The battle, when it started . . . We were waiting for it . . . We weren't prepared. They had tanks. Machine guns. More men. Ours went down like ninepins.' He shuddered. 'We had no chance. We had no cover. We collapsed . . .'

'How did you manage to get back to England?' asked Jim Blake.

'I was lucky. I managed to crawl away. Perhaps I shouldn't have . . . Some of them might think I was a coward but I wouldn't have been any help. An old man took me into his house and cleaned my wounds and let me stay two nights. It was a risk for him but he said he was too old to care. Then a friend of his gave me a lift going north . . .' Angus collapsed back on to the sofa. He had said enough.

'Well, I am glad you have come to our house,' said Isabella.

'We all are,' added her mother.

'You are kind, Mrs Blake . . .' His voice faded again.

'We are only too pleased to help you, a friend of William's . . .' Her voice too petered out and she locked her hands together in her lap. She turned her head to the side as if she were trying to hold back tears.

'Where is your home, Angus?' asked Isabella. She could tell from his voice that he was not from London. Scotland, she thought. Another one. Would he die too?

She felt chilled in spite of the hot fire that roared up the chimney.

'I don't have one.'

'You don't? No family at all?'

'My mother is dead.'

'And your father?'

'He doesn't want to see me.'

'Not at all?'

'Never. Last time I saw him he threw my stuff out into the street.'

There was silence in the room for a moment and then Isabella spoke again. 'Was it because you were going to Spain?'

He nodded. 'He thought I was an idiot. He said –' Angus paused before going on – 'if I was such a fool, I was no son of his. He's a lawyer. I have disappointed him.'

Isabella wanted to ask him why he *did* go to Spain? Was it because it was an adventure or did he really care about the country, even further away from home? She understood why William had gone, but there were so many young men from all over Britain who had gone to fight for the Republican cause who had never set foot in the country before.

'My father wouldn't give a damn if I was alive or dead,' muttered Angus. 'Better dead.'

'I can't believe it,' cried Isabella's mother. 'His own son!'

'I can,' said Angus. 'I know him.'

'He must be a hard man then.'

'He is.'

'You must stay with us until you recover, Angus,' said Jim Blake.

'But you don't know me!'

'We know you now. And you are a friend of our son. Even if you were not, we wouldn't turn you out.'

'Besides,' added his wife, 'you went to fight for my country.'

'You are very kind,' Angus repeated. His voice was fading again and he slumped back, exhausted.

Maria Blake got up and went over to put her hand on his forehead. 'No *bueno*!' She shook her head. 'Jim, I think we need the doctor.'

Suddenly Isabella noticed that Arthur was standing at the back of the room. They hadn't heard him come in, but by the look on his face he must have been there for some time. His arms were folded across his chest. She had a good idea what he would be thinking. Why should every Tom, Dick and Harry be foisted on to us? This house is like a refugee camp. He would have to share his bedroom with yet another stranger. It was not a big room. The beds were almost touching each other and there was space only for one upright chair.

Isabella remembered the armband in Arthur's drawer. She must try to talk some sense into his head before it was too late. Perhaps it was too late even now. She looked over at him. His face was impassive.

'Isabella,' said her father, 'go, dear, and see if Dr Gebler is at home?'

'Yes, Papa.' She left at once. It was cold and wet and dark outside. She pulled up her collar, ran head down, and went straight into Sean's arms.

'Whoa! Where are you going? I have good news, Issie!' Sean lifted her off her feet and whirled her round. 'I've got a promotion. Is that not the best thing you ever heard? I'm to work in Stores! My brothers are dead jealous!' He laughed.

'That's great, Sean,' Isabella gasped, trying to catch her breath and sound pleased for him. She could think only of William. Where was he at this moment? Had he been wounded? Was he alive? Or dead? His friend had managed to escape after the battle and get back to Britain. Had William? Perhaps he was on his way. Then again, perhaps not. Her head rocked with all these conflicting thoughts and there was Sean standing in front of her, as pleased as Punch, grinning from ear to ear. But then he didn't know about Angus.

'I'm going to take you out tonight, Issie!' he said. 'We'll have ourselves a good time.'

'Not tonight I'm afraid, Sean.' Isabella told him about Angus and watched as his happiness fizzled out. 'I'm really sorry.'

'Not your fault, for the love of God!'

'I must go now. Fetch the doctor.'

'Of course.' He released her.

Dr Gebler was at home eating his evening meal. He put down his knife and fork straight away, wiped his mouth on his starched white napkin and came with her, leaving his wife sighing and shaking her head.

'I'm sorry,' said Isabella.

'Don't be,' said Dr Gebler. She had to slow her steps on the way back. Dr Gebler was limping badly tonight.

They came in to find Angus lying with his head lolling backwards and his eyes half closed.

'Thank you for coming, Doctor,' said Maria Blake.

'I think we'll leave you to it, Dr Gebler,' said her husband.

They retreated to the scullery. There was no sign of Arthur. Isabella put the kettle on and made a pot of tea.

'I hope he's not going to die like Robbie,' said her mother, crossing herself. 'After everything he's been through. Seems it was the Red Cross that helped him in the end. Somebody was round the street last week collecting for them. I gave them a shilling.'

'Have some tea, Mama,' said Isabella. 'I've put two sugars in for you.'

Her mother was not overly fond of tea, preferring coffee, but she drank it since everybody else did. All along the street whenever there was a hint of a crisis they would light the gas and put the kettle on.

They drank their tea and waited.

'Sean's going to work in Stores,' said Isabella after a while.

'That's good,' said her father. 'He deserves it. He's a good lad. He works hard.'

They fell silent again, and didn't move until they heard the living-room door open. They jumped up and went to meet Dr Gebler.

'The lad is obviously exhausted and dehydrated and suffers pain from the amputation on his hand, but his pulse is not too bad.' The doctor reached into his black bag. 'I think he will have been a strong, well-nourished boy before be was wounded.'

Isabella's dad asked about Angus's leg, which had also suffered a wound.

Dr Gebler nodded, frowning, and explained that it would need watching. He had taken off the bandages and dressed it. Angus had a nasty infection in the hip too. 'If any of the wounds deteriorate I'll get an ambulance to take him along to the hospital.' He sighed. 'Why must all this go on and on? Most of us want a quiet life.'

'Because men like Franco want to be dictators and rule the world,' said Jim Blake quietly.

'Ah yes. And Herr Hitler too.'

Jim Blake nodded.

'Give him these painkillers and plenty of water,' said Dr Gebler, 'and I will come back in the morning. But if he deteriorates in any way do not hesitate to call me.'

'We are very grateful, Doctor,' said Maria Blake. 'You must be tired by night.'

'A bit,' he acknowledged with a rueful smile.

'What do I owe you?' asked Jim Blake. 'I must pay you this time.'

'Certainly not!' said Dr Gebler, and left.

Eighteen

When Isabella went into work next day she found Madge all agog. Once they were at their desks she leaned over towards Isabella and whispered behind her hand, 'I went to that meeting last night!' She sounded excited.

'Tell me later,' said Isabella. The supervisor had her eye fixed on them. There was work to do and no time for chatting.

At lunchtime the girls found a secluded corner where they could eat their sandwiches.

'Well,' said Isabella, 'what did you think of the meeting?'

'I thought it was a good meeting,' said Madge primly, and then warming up, added, 'He's ever such an interesting speaker.'

'Rupert?'

He's so well spoken. Everybody applauded him except for a couple of hooligans at the back. But they got short shrift!'

'In what way?'

'They was asked to leave,' Madge giggled. 'Couple of bruisers saw them out. They ended up on their backsides on the pavement. It was quite a laugh. Well, serves them right, doesn't it? They'd just come to make trouble. They were asking for it.'

'So what about Rupert then?' Isabella felt uncomfortable asking, but she wanted to know.

'I thought everything he said was absolutely right!' Madge's face was flushed as if she were still at the meeting.

'What *did* he say?'

'That we should make our country strong.'

'In what way?' asked Isabella.

'That we should keep England for ourselves. Do you know that's just what my dad's been saying for years? We've let too many foreigners in. Well, they're everywhere, aren't they? In the East End 'specially. Maybe not in Hampstead and those places. The toffs know how to look after themselves. You should see our street!' Madge was getting worked up now. 'We've got Ities and Paddies and God knows what, even blacks. From Africa. And then there's the Jews!'

'Yes, there's the Jews! Hitler's persecuting them in Germany. They have no choice but to leave their homes. You must have heard.'

'How do you know?' Madge looked put out by Isabella's outburst.

175

'We listen to the BBC.'

'The BBC,' scoffed Madge. 'Rupert says you can't believe everything you hear on the BBC. What are all these people doing here? Why don't they go home to where they belong?'

Madge might as well have been up on a soapbox herself preaching at Hyde Park Corner on a Sunday. She'd been a good candidate for Rupert to recruit. Isabella took a deep breath and controlled her temper.

'My mum's Spanish,' she said. 'One hundred per cent. *Her* mum was a gypsy.'

'A *gypsy*?' Madge looked horrified. 'We had some gypsies snooping about in the summer. Offering to sharpen knives.'

Isabella did not respond.

'My dad told them to skedaddle,' said Madge. 'They're light fingered. Stole the washing off the line from our next-door neighbour. Police caught them,' she ended on a note of triumph.

'Couple of local kids in our street were nicked last week for stealing,' said Isabella steadily. 'They were English.'

Madge wasn't going to come back on that one. Instead she said, 'Still can't believe your gran was a gypsy!'

'Yes, she was. Still is. She was born in a cave.' Isabella saw the incredulous look on Madge's face. She'd wanted to shock her and she had succeeded.

'You're havin' me on!' said Madge. 'Who's ever heard of anyone being born in a *cave*?'

'It's true, cross my heart! My grandmother was really and truly born in a cave in Granada.'

'Never 'eard of it.'

'It's in Andalucia, that's in the south of Spain,' Isabella went on. 'Lots of gypsies live there. They're great flamenco singers and dancers.'

Madge was looking uncomfortable. 'But your own mum wasn't, was she?' she said, glancing away to avoid Isabella's sparking dark eyes. 'Born in a cave? I mean, she got married to your dad.'

'You think he wouldn't have married her if she'd been born in a cave?'

'Oh, how do I know?' Madge shrugged. Then she pondered for a moment. 'That means you're –?'

'Part gypsy? Yes. My mum's a half so that means I'm a quarter.'

'Must say you do look quite dark. I'd wondered.'

'And my best friends are Irish,' Isabella went on, having now got her teeth into the argument.

'Why did they come over here?'

'To get work. There was no work for them in Ireland.'

'You see, they take jobs away from our boys!' Madge livened up again, pleased to have made her point. 'That's what Rupert was saying! Why should they be allowed to do that?'

Isabella took a deep breath and then decided to leave it there otherwise they'd end up in a full-blown shouting match. Even now heads had turned towards them. She drank some water to cool herself down.

'So you think Rupert talks sense, do you?' she asked.

Madge hardly needed to answer. Her glowing face showed it all. 'He's got such lovely manners. The perfect gent. You don't meet many of those these days. He's asked me if I'd like to come along to their next meeting and help out.'

'And would you?' asked Isabella.

'Well, why not?'

'He's a Blackshirt. D'you know what that is? A Fascist. He follows Oswald Mosley, who supports Adolf Hitler.'

'So what?' demanded Madge.

Isabella was floored for a moment. She didn't know anyone who thought Hitler was all right. Except Rupert. And maybe Arthur, but he said nothing. He was closed up like a clam these days. Whenever her father criticised Hitler and said he needed watching, that he had ambitions to conquer Europe, any fool could see it, Arthur would leave the room.

'Rupert says all sorts of high-up people support them,' Madge went on. 'People with titles. Dukes even. Oh yes, I'm not fibbing! They're not riffraff. You're just prejudiced. You won't listen to another point of view. That's exactly what Rupert says!'

'I wouldn't pay too much attention to what Rupert says if I were you.'

'Are you jealous?' asked Madge.

'*Jealous*? Certainly not!' retorted Isabella.

Madge smiled, like the cat that has got the cream. Only there was no cream to be got, Isabella felt sure of that. Madge wouldn't listen, though, if she were to say so.

It was time to get back to their desks. Just as well, thought Isabella. She felt like thumping Madge.

When they emerged after work into the fresh air, the first person they saw was Rupert. He was leaning against the same wall, a picture of relaxed confidence.

Isabella took a step back, Madge one forward.

'Rupert!' she cried.

Rupert met her with a smile on his face and an outstretched hand, which Madge was quick to take. 'It's ever so nice to see you again, Rupert.'

He looked over her shoulder at Isabella. 'Good evening, Miss Isabella.'

She didn't bother to reply.

'Issie's in a bad mood,' giggled Madge. She wasn't letting go of Rupert's hand. 'We've been having words about your Mr Mosley and his Blackshirts.'

Isabella didn't wait to hear Rupert's reply. 'See you tomorrow, Madge,' she said and went striding on, breaking into a run when she saw a bus coming.

There was no sign of Angus when she arrived home. The sofa was empty.

'Where is he?' she cried. Surely it was not going to be like Robbie all over again! She could never forget that some family in Glasgow would be wondering where their son was. She had never managed to trace them. In the end, her dad and some of his mates at work had clubbed together and paid for Robbie to have a decent burial.

'Dr Gebler had Angus taken along to the hospital this afternoon,' said her mother from the scullery. 'He thought it better to play safe.'

'Play safe,' muttered Isabella. Nothing seemed safe any longer. She had dreamed the previous night about William. She saw him running with an aeroplane like a giant moth hovering over his head, diving for cover into a thorn bush. She just knew it was a bush of thorns. She heard his cry as he fell in and then she had wakened, trembling, a cry on her own lips.

Her mother had heard her and came into her room to put her arms round her. 'You've been having a nightmare, love. But everything is going to be all right.'

Isabella knew that not to be true, but for the moment it comforted her to think so and feel the security of her mother's arms.

Nineteen

There was a certain coolness between Isabella and Madge after their conversation about Rupert's meeting. They kept their old desks – one couldn't really ask for a move – and they were perfectly polite to each other. But Isabella started going out at lunchtime now that spring was here and the weather improving. She ate her sandwiches on a park bench or a low wall. She couldn't stay out for long but even a short break in the fresh air was welcome. It helped clear her head.

Madge soon struck up a friendship with a girl called Daisy. They went around arm in arm and whispered to each other. Sometimes as they whispered they looked over at Isabella. She would stare back at them until they dropped their gaze.

One day when she was in a cubicle in the ladies room she heard Madge's voice. She was talking to someone but it wasn't Daisy.

'I'm telling you, cross my heart, it's true!'

'Honest?'

'She told me herself. She's a quarter. Her mother's a half. But even so! Don't you think she looks kind of dark-skinned?'

'I'd never really thought –'

'Darker than us English girls anyway.'

'I suppose. You wouldn't think they'd take on –'

Isabella had heard enough. She burst open the door of the cubicle and confronted them. The other girl looked embarrassed, Madge did not. She tilted her chin defiantly.

'Finished your little chat, have you?' asked Isabella. 'You're a rat, Madge! You should do well with the Fascists. What's more, you're stupid! Rupert will use you and dump you in the gutter.'

'How dare you speak to me like that!'

Madge moved a step closer to Isabella and raised her hand as if about to slap her face. Then she hesitated, as if she knew that it might be a foolish move. Isabella, who was taller by half a head and had been brought up with two brothers, showed by her stance that she would have the advantage. Madge had told Isabella she was an only child and the apple of her father's eye. 'He lets me get away with murder,' she'd bragged.

Isabella faced Madge full on now. Madge retreated. Then she left the room, followed by the other girl.

She hadn't been warned off, though. When Isabella was leaving work at the end of the day she saw Madge in a huddle with three or four other girls. There was no doubt what she was talking about. She lifted her head and gave Isabella a sly smile. She had protection round her now. The others in the group turned their heads too, and stared at Isabella.

Isabella put her back to them and walked off briskly in the direction of her bus stop, her head held high. But she passed the bus stop and kept on going. She needed to work off her anger. She felt shaken, of course she did, she couldn't pretend she didn't. Anyone would. The stares had been so hard, so unfriendly. Yet only yesterday she had been chatting with two of those girls. She had no doubt that the gossip would be all round the place by next morning, and magnified. It would be like a game of Chinese Whispers when you sit in a ring and pass a whisper around. By the time it gets back to you the message is totally distorted.

On her way home she decided to call in at the hospital to ask about Angus. By the time she got there she had calmed down. Her mother said always to count to ten, in Spanish of course, and then you would feel better. Isabella had had to go way beyond ten to achieve that. But the news at the hospital was encouraging. Angus was more than holding his own. The wounds where his fingers had been amputated had miraculously not gone septic, nor had the ones in his leg. His temperature was almost normal and he'd taken a little food. Isabella asked a nurse if she could see him.

'You a relative?'

'No. But he came to our house. He's a friend of my brother's and he hasn't got any family in London.'

'Don't stay too long then,' said the nurse. 'You'll tire him. In spite of his improvement he has had some really bad nightmares. Every time he drops off. Wakes up screaming. Not surprising, after what he's been through, is it?'

'No,' agreed Isabella, 'it's not.'

'Sounds dreadful. All those young men. He's been telling us about it. Sounds like hell on earth. Hope it doesn't start up over here!'

'I hope not too!' Isabella couldn't help picturing William, injured, bleeding, alone.

'He's in the end bed on the left-hand side,' said the nurse.

Angus was awake. He gave Isabella a small smile.

'It's Is—?' He hesitated.

'Isabella. But you can call me Issie.'

He nodded and tried to pull himself up against the pillows. Isabella went to help him, putting her hands under his armpits. He winced and his face contorted with pain.

'Are you all right?' she asked anxiously. 'Have I hurt your back?'

'No, no! I'm fine.' His voice croaked, yet was surprisingly strong.

She pulled up a chair closer to the bed.

'That's better!' he said. 'I can see you properly now. You look nice. You do! William talked a lot about you.'

'He was always my favourite brother from when I was little. He told me stories and he looked out for me in the street. I was always safe when William was around. We are very close.' Isabella thought of Arthur and felt a small pang. Perhaps he'd felt left out.

'William told me you were very pretty. He was right.'

Isabella felt herself blushing. She asked, 'So how are you feeling now?'

'Bit rough.'

'You must be!'

'William?' asked Angus. 'Any sign of –?'

She shook her head. 'No.'

'It wouldn't surprise me if he were to turn up out of the blue. Well, I did, didn't I?'

Yes, but Angus hadn't seen William at all after the bombardment.

They chatted a little. Isabella didn't ask Angus about Spain even though she longed to. He veered away from the topic. He asked her what she did in her spare time. 'Do you like going to the pictures?'

'Oh yes!'

'Maybe I could take you out sometime, when they release me?'

'Maybe,' she said, or maybe not. It would upset Sean if she were to go with Angus. 'I must get home now though. Else I'll be late for dinner.'

Angus didn't want her to leave. 'Stay a little longer,' he pleaded, and so she did.

'It's all right,' she said, getting up when she saw the nurse advancing on them. 'I'm just going.'

'Thanks for coming, Issie,' said Angus. 'You will come again, won't you?'

She nodded and left.

On the way down her street she glanced in at the Flynns' window. The light was on in the room and the curtains were open. They always were. Sean saw her and came bounding out.

'You're late? Where have you been?'

She told him and he went quiet.

'What's up with you?' asked Isabella.

'Nothing.' He shrugged.

'Don't tell me you're jealous,' she snapped. She was tired, she needed some food.

'Don't talk daft!' retorted Sean. 'You were long enough, mind. I've been watching out for you.'

'Honestly, Sean Flynn!' Isabella tossed her head and carried on to her own door. It wasn't often he annoyed her, but she couldn't be bothered with him this evening.

Her mum and dad and Arthur were well through their meal.

'You're late,' said her mum.

'I know! Sorry.'

She told them where she had been, and her mother went to fetch her dinner. They were having stew made with scrag end of mutton with dough balls. It was tasty and Isabella was hungry. She felt better once she had eaten.

Arthur asked permission to leave the table.

'Where are you off to?' asked his father.

Arthur shrugged. 'Nowhere special. The gym maybe.'

'Which one?' asked Isabella.

'Don't know yet.' He turned away from her.

After Arthur had gone his father said thoughtfully, 'He's moody these days. Not got much to say for himself either. Any idea what he's up to?' He looked at his daughter, who shrugged.

'He doesn't talk to me,' Isabella said, gathering up the dirty plates. 'I'll do the dishes, Mama.' She took them through to the scullery, filled the kettle and put it on the range to boil, gazing out into the darkness of the back yard, lit only by the streak of light coming from their window. When she heard a movement behind her she turned her head to see her father coming in. He picked up a tea towel.

'I'll dry for you,' he said.

'You don't have to.'

'I know I don't have to. But maybe I want to.'

Jim Blake was unlike other dads who wouldn't touch 'women's work'. Mr Flynn was one. 'What have I got a wife fer?' he'd say. His wife would just shrug and say he was useless. She was not a lot better herself. Bridie was the one left with the chores in that house, though the boys would fill the coal scuttle and lug it in, and when there were no clean dishes left they'd wash them. They'd been known to wash their own socks too, especially if they were going dancing on a Saturday night.

'I thought you'd something on your mind, Issie, when you came in,' said her dad.

She shrugged, keeping her back to him. 'I was thinking about William, after seeing Angus in the hospital.'

'Why don't you turn around so as I can see you?'

She turned slowly.

'What is it?' asked her dad.

Isabella told him about Madge. 'What annoys me most is that I've let her upset me!'

'Come here,' said her dad. He hung up the tea towel and put his arms around her. 'Of course it's upset you! Why wouldn't it when someone's trying to turn people against you? I don't think, though, that you needed to go on about your grandmother being born in a cave.'

'I know,' she admitted.

'It's true, of course, and nothing to be ashamed of, but

it's just that those people don't understand how some others live.'

She nodded. 'I won't say anything to Mama.'

'No, don't. It might upset her. And when you go in to work tomorrow, just hold your head up and look them in the eye!'

Twenty

In the morning, arriving at work, Isabella felt a bit queasy, then she remembered her father's advice. She held her head up as she entered the building and smiled, or said, 'Good morning' to everyone she passed. She met a couple of girls who goggled at her and then covered their mouths with their hands and went into a fit of the giggles. *Let them!* She wasn't going to allow it to bother her. But that was easier said than done, of course. Another girl, coming behind the first two, turned her head to the side, embarrassed. Madge had obviously been to work. When she herself arrived, she made a point of dramatically turning her back on Isabella. Why on earth did Rupert bother with her? Whatever he was, he was not stupid. And Madge was!

Isabella found out the reason that Saturday night. She was performing at the Queen's Theatre in Poplar with her mother again. When they arrived, there was Madge, along with another girl from the office, working the queue, heads bent, talking earnestly to each person in turn, handing out leaflets. And now along came Rupert, dressed in a black blazer with gold buttons, giving both of them a pat on the back as he passed. Madge looked up at him and smiled. Isabella wasn't close enough to tell if her face was flushed or not but felt sure that it would be.

'What's he doing here?' muttered Sean, who had Rupert in his sight line.

'Just stay away from him, Sean, please!' urged Isabella.

'He's got Rupert on the brain,' said Bridie. She sighed. 'He keeps going on about him. I've told him you'd never go off with a Blackshirt.'

Rupert came into the performance and stood in his usual place at the back of the hall. The girls were left outside in the cold to continue their 'good work'. Earlier that week Isabella's dad had read reports that support for the British Union of Fascists had been declining, and that they'd done badly in the recent London County Council elections. Perhaps they were working extra hard to try to keep up membership numbers.

Apparently some supporters were beginning to think that Hitler might not be such a good thing after all. Why they ever had was beyond Isabella! Even some of the BUF supporters with titles who, she thought, might have more sense.

Not necessarily, said her father. Perhaps just the opposite. Hitler was becoming more and more threatening in Europe. They sometimes listened to the rant of his voice on the wireless. Not that they could understand German. They didn't need to. And on the newsreel at the cinema they saw his armies marching stiff-legged, right arms extended in front of them in salute. The sight of them gave Isabella the shivers. What if they were to come over here and invade London? Lots of people were talking about that. They said that if the Nazis came here they'd change all the street names into German and everybody would have to speak German. That would be the least of it, Isabella's father said. He often reminded the family that not all Germans would want to wage war against them, especially those who remembered the war of 1914 to 1918.

More Jews were arriving all the time in the East End from different parts of Europe, Germany and Austria in particular. They brought with them tales of their friends and relatives disappearing in the night. Some had been helped in their escape by non-Jewish Germans. One group had just moved into a house a few doors along from the Blakes where another Jewish family was already lodged. Isabella's mother had given her a bag of food to take along to the newcomers but Arthur said they'd probably turn their noses up at Christian food.

'Not if they are hungry!' said his mother.

'I heard they'd starve first.'

'People say too much!' snapped his mother. 'Go, Isabella, take it!'

A small elderly man with a long white beard opened the door to Isabella. He greeted her courteously and accepted the bag with many thanks in poor English.

Mrs Flynn was leaning up against her door yawning as Isabella came by. She told her she was fed up with all this war talk. 'What's the point of worrying? Probably never happen. But you know, maybe they *are* letting too many furreners in.' She'd nodded in the direction of the house Isabella had just visited.

Isabella tried to avoid looking in Rupert's direction at the back of the Queen's Theatre that evening, but she couldn't help catching sight of him two or three times during the dance. The look she gave him was defiant, matching the music.

'*Olé!*' cried the guitarist as he began to play. As Isabella twirled, her flounced skirt swirling around her legs, she stamped her heels vigorously and tossed her head. Her dad had once observed that flamenco dancing must be a good way to get rid of pent-up emotions. Isabella certainly had plenty of them. At the end of their performance she saw Rupert raise his hands high above his head, clapping steadily and rhythmically until the audience quietened.

When they came out of the theatre afterwards they

found two men at the stage door rattling tins.

'Please help the Republican cause in Spain!' they begged. 'Our government ain't helpin' them. Franco's getting money from Hitler and Mussolini. Please help.'

There didn't seem to be much money in the tins. People had little to spare these days. Jim Blake dug deep into his pockets and Isabella and her mother donated part of their performance fee. Sean found a shilling in his trouser pocket but Bridie could only come up with tuppence ha'penny. They talked for a few minutes to the men. One of them had a son who had gone out to fight and been killed at the battle of Jarama, so his father had heard via the Red Cross. He had tears in his eyes as he told them and had to take the big blue-spotted handkerchief from his top pocket and blow his nose forcefully.

'We'd like his body back. Not much to ask, is it? We don't want him in a mass grave.'

They commiserated and told the men about Angus and William.

'God bless them both,' said the one who had lost his son. 'And may He bring back your boy William to you safe and sound.'

'Amen to that,' said William's mother, touching the bereaved man on the arm. 'I will remember your son in my prayers.'

Her mother had a long list of people to pray for, thought Isabella, and it was growing longer by the day.

It was a wonder she could remember all their names. Top of the list of course was William, followed by numerous members of the family in Spain whom they hadn't heard from for months. Sisters, brothers, nephews, nieces, cousins, second cousins. They still didn't know where any of them had ended up after leaving Malaga, or even if they were alive or dead.

And then there was Angus lying in his hospital bed. Isabella's dad had called at the hospital to be told that he had, after all, contracted an infection. Her mother had always mistrusted hospitals. She was convinced the air was full of germs and no matter how much they scrubbed the place down with carbolic soap they wouldn't get rid of them. She had given birth to her three children at home, like most women, and had not had a bit of trouble. Those who had to be hospitalised due to complications usually came back home with some kind of infection or other.

The Blakes said goodnight to the two men and prepared to move on.

'Thank you, sir. Thank you, mam,' they cried, doffing their caps.

There was no sign of either Rupert or Madge, and Isabella was thankful for that. So was Sean. She saw him taking a long look up ahead and then relaxing. She slid her hand into his and tucked the other one into the crook of Bridie's arm. Walking close, all three together, they were protected from the wind. If only William could have been there, closing in the end of their group on the other side of Bridie, the evening would have been nigh on perfect.

The next day, Sunday, Isabella's mother asked her to come and visit Angus at the hospital after lunch.

While they were getting ready Sean knocked on the front door and put his head round. 'Are you there, Issie?' he called out.

'Come on in, Sean,' said her mother.

'It's a nice day, isn't it, Mrs Blake?' Sean looked at Isabella. 'I was thinking we might go to the park?'

'Later maybe, Sean,' said Isabella. 'We're going to the hospital first, to see Angus.'

'Oh,' said Sean.

It annoyed her, the way he said it. Angus needed visitors. He had been brave and gone to fight in Spain, and he'd been wounded. Did she think that Sean should have gone? She wasn't sure. She was proud of William for doing it but wished with all her heart that he had not.

'You could come with us, Sean,' said her mother.

'I don't think they let more than two visitors in at a time, Mama,' put in Isabella.

'He wouldn't be wanting to see me, anyway,' said Sean. 'I don't know the fella. I'll see you later, Issie.' He backed out.

Angus was in a small side room that stank of disinfectant.

He looked happy to see them and did his best to sit up but after a couple of tries gave up and slid back down the pillows. The visitors were unable to help. The nurse had warned them to stay well clear of him, they didn't want him to pick up their germs.

They'd brought him a bar of Fry's cream chocolate, which made him smile, though he didn't try to open it. Isabella saw a big change in him from her previous visit. They didn't stay long, the nurse saw to that.

'See you soon,' said Isabella as they were leaving.

Angus nodded and closed his eyes. They left him to sleep.

'Mama, I hope we do see Angus soon,' said Isabella, as they left the hospital.

'We will return soon, and I will pray for him.'

Isabella said nothing. She used to find her mother's prayers a comfort but was less convinced of their powers these days.

They were glad to be back out in the fresh air. The day was mild with a soft wind. It would be nice in the park. Perhaps she would go for a walk with Sean later.

When they got home and she told her father that Angus was not so good he looked thoughtful. 'I wonder if we should contact his father,' he said.

'But Dad,' said Isabella, 'they don't speak. Remember?'

'Yes, but Angus's father should be told. He is a lawyer in Edinburgh. What we need is a phone book.'

Twenty one

In the two telephone boxes nearest them the directories were missing. Isabella said she would go to the library straight from work the next day and ask for help.

'We don't know his Christian name,' she told the librarian, 'but his surname is Anderson and he is a lawyer in Edinburgh.'

'That shouldn't be too difficult.'

Within minutes the librarian had found a listing under the name of Roderick Abernethy Anderson, complete with home and business addresses and a telephone number for both.

'That could be him then!' said Isabella, amazed how quick and easy the search had been compared to her frustrating search for Robbie's family.

'That's because your Mr Anderson is a lawyer,' said the librarian. 'A businessman. Your friend Robbie's was quite a different story, from what we know of him, poor lad. The further up you are in the world, the easier it is to be found. The lower down, the easier it is to drop from sight.'

Isabella took down Mr Anderson's details and ran home eager to show them to her father.

'We'll go out to the telephone box after we've eaten,' he said, 'and see how far we can get. I changed a shilling and sixpence for coppers at Mrs McGill's when I was passing but I've no idea how much a call will cost to Scotland. Could be a fair bit, being long distance.'

Isabella turned out her pockets and found a few pence. Her mother also fished three pennies out of the corners of her old, sagging, Spanish leather purse.

At their nearest phone box there was a short queue. Three people in all, and one inside already making a call. No one spoke for long, however, and soon it was their turn. They stepped inside the box and Isabella pulled the door shut behind them, wrinkling her nose. The box stank of stale cigarette smoke. Her dad lifted the receiver and dialled zero for the operator.

'I would like to make a call to Scotland. It's an Edinburgh number . . .' He gave the number, waited, with the coins cradled in his left hand, ready to insert them in the slot when directed, and said to Isabella, who was hovering anxiously, 'The operator is trying to connect me.' A moment or two later, he added, 'I can hear it ringing.'

But nobody answered. The operator came back on the line to tell him to try later.

'Thank you,' said her dad into the receiver.

They decided to go for a walk. The evening was fine and the moon almost full. Isabella took her dad's arm. He asked about her work and how she was getting on with Madge.

Isabella shrugged. 'I just ignore her.'

'Best thing.'

Her dad went on to say he'd been thinking that she should go back to evening classes and get some more qualifications. He wished he'd had the chance. He'd had to leave school at twelve to help the family's coffers.

'You should do the Matric, love. You're a bright girl. It's a wide world out there, you know!'

Isabella had been thinking about it herself. 'I might go along in the autumn when they start their new classes.'

While she wasn't working, she had begun to learn Spanish with her mother. She had always known a few words and phrases but not taken it much beyond that. She had enjoyed improving her knowledge of the language now that she was a little older. When Franco was beaten and the war over they would go back to Spain, declared her mother, and have a wonderful holiday visiting everybody.

'Let's give Angus's father another go, shall we?' suggested her dad.

There was no queue at the telephone box now.

'Somebody in it, though,' said Isabella.

There seemed to be some kind of scuffle going on inside the box, then the door was flung open and out came two boys on the run. Her dad caught hold of the collar of one of them and swung him round. The other showed a clean pair of heels and was gone into the night.

'Mickey,' cried Isabella, 'what were you doing in there?'

'Nuttin',' he muttered.

He wriggled and Jim Blake released him but blocked his escape. 'What were you up to, Mickey?'

Mickey shrugged. 'Just lookin'. Sometimes people forget –' He shrugged.

'To get their money back?'

'That's their fault then, innit? If they don't press the button. Up to them. If they leave it lyin' anybody can have it. There was nothin' tonight.'

Isabella understood Mickey's point of view. She remembered that when they were younger she and Bridie used to go round checking the boxes. Sometimes people might have dropped the odd coin or two on the floor. They used to reckon that there was no way you could track them down so they might as well pick up the money and keep it for themselves.

'Is that all you were doing in there, Mickey?' asked Jim

Blake. 'Sounded like you were fighting over something. What's that you've got in there?'

'Nothin'.' Mickey put a protective hand over his jacket pocket.

'Let's have a look.'

Mickey didn't resist. Isabella's father withdrew a crumpled but full packet of twenty Players cigarettes from his pocket.

'Have you been thieving in Mrs McGill's, Mickey?' asked Jim Blake. 'She's got to earn a living, you know. She's not well off and Mr McGill can't work on account of his lung disease.'

Mickey stood with his head hanging down, ready to take off the first chance he got. His legs were braced and his eyes, though lowered, were alert.

'I won't tell your father,' said Jim Blake. 'Not this time.'

Mickey lifted his head. 'He wouldn't give a toss.'

'The law would, though. Off you go!'

'Can I have the fags back?' Mickey held out his hand.

'Sorry.'

'Aw, Mr Blake! Please! I was goin' to give some to me mum. What are you going' to do wid them?'

'Put them in the bin.'

'No! You can't do that! It'd be a waste.'

He was right, of course, thought Isabella, but she knew her dad.

'Me mum was fair gaspin' for a fag earlier and she's

got nothin' left in her purse,' Mickey went on. He was good at putting on a whine. 'Me da had stole what was in there to go to the pub.'

The argument was terminated by the arrival of PC MacDade.

'Evening.' The constable eyed Mickey. 'No trouble I take it, Mr Blake?'

'No, nothing. Away you go home then, Mickey!'

The constable watched him go. 'He sails close to the wind, that lad.'

Jim Blake sighed. 'You're right.' He opened the door of the telephone box. 'We're just going in to make a call.'

'I'll leave you to get on with it then.'

The constable resumed his patrol and Isabella and her father stepped into the box. This time they were lucky and the call went through. Her father raised his thumb.

Isabella was excited. She wished she could hear the voice at the other end of the line.

'My name is Jim Blake,' said her dad, 'and I'm phoning from London . . . Yes, London. It's about your son, Angus.' There seemed to be silence at the other end now. He carried on, 'Angus is seriously ill in hospital, here in London –' He broke off while he listened and then continued – 'I'm sorry to hear that, Mr Anderson, but please would you just let me give you the details in case you change your mind?' He waited. 'Thank you. Your son is in Mile End hospital. That's in Bancroft Road, which is off Mile End Road, in the East End of the city. I do hope, sir, that you will come.' The call was terminated at the other end and Jim Blake replaced the receiver.

'What did he say?' asked Isabella.

'Not a lot. He didn't commit himself one way or the other. Let's hope he comes. I don't know how a father can turn his back on a son – or a daughter,' he added, smiling at Isabella. 'What could be important enough to cause such a rift?'

She thought of Arthur with Mosley's Blackshirts. It was like a time bomb waiting to explode. Her father had asked her two or three times recently if she knew where Arthur went in the evenings. He was becoming suspicious.

She took his arm and they set off back home. It was a cold night so there were few people on the street but the pubs were busy. Money might be scarce but some men seemed to be able to find money for beer if nothing else.

'Well, did you find Angus's father?' asked Isabella's mother as soon as they set foot in the house. Her husband told her how the phone call had gone. 'You tell me he doesn't want to see his son? *Madre Mia*! What a hard man! He must be pitied.'

'Well, we shall see,' said her husband. 'You never know, he might change his mind.'

'I shall pray for him.'

It was only when she was getting ready for bed that Isabella remembered the cigarettes in her father's pocket.

He was in possession of stolen goods! Not that the police were going to be coming round to search their house. Still, she must get rid of them. The living-room fire was still smouldering.

All was quiet overhead. She slipped out into the hall where their coats hung from a row of pegs. As she put her hand into her father's pocket and withdrew the cigarettes the front door opened and in came Arthur.

He looked at the packet in her hand. 'What are you doing with that? Don't tell me you've started to smoke on the sly!'

'Of course not.'

They retreated to the living room and she started to explain how the cigarettes had come to be in their possession when Arthur cut across saying, 'Father shouldn't protect petty thieves!'

'But Mickey is only eleven.'

'He's old enough to know he is breaking the law.'

'But –'

'But nothing! He should be made to face the music or he'll never learn. He should be brought to court and punished. What kind of society are we creating when we let criminals get away with it? No wonder the country's in such a mess!'

'But his parents . . .'

'So they're rotten parents. And they're immigrants –'

Isabella snapped. 'Oh, shut up! Keep your Fascist talk

to yourself! Keep it for your pal Rupert and Mr Mosley! Put your black shirt on and your armband and do a few goose steps up and down the hall and salute Adolf Hitler!' She was aware she was shouting. She raised her own arm Nazi-style.

He stared at her. 'How do you know?'

'You must think I'm stupid!'

Their father's voice reached them from the landing above. 'What's going on down there?' He didn't wait for an answer but came running down the stairs.

Isabella looked away from her brother, who had turned his head and was staring into the fading embers of the fire, his lips pursed.

'Now then,' demanded their father, 'what was all the shouting about?'

Isabella said nothing.

Arthur lifted his head. 'Father, I have something to tell you.' He paused and Isabella held her breath. 'I am a member of the BUF,' Arthur went on, 'and I am not ashamed of it. I know you will disapprove but I believe what they stand for to be right and just. They care about England and want to protect it. What can be wrong with that? To protect your own country?' His voice now became passionate. 'We are much maligned and misrepresented.' He spoke as if he were standing on a platform in front of a crowd and had rehearsed the words.

Jim Blake was staring at his son in disbelief. 'You cannot be serious,' he said, even though it was obvious Arthur meant what he said. He had spoken passionately. This was not something to be joked about. 'So you are telling me that you are a *Fascist*? I can't believe it. My son a *Fascist*!'

'You can't cope with it, can you?' Arthur replied. 'That I want to go my own way? That I don't want to follow yours? But I can think for myself!' He jabbed himself in the chest with his forefinger.

Jim Blake sat down in his old leather chair. He frowned as if puzzled, as if he could not quite take in what his son, his own flesh and blood, was saying. His face paled. Isabella went over to him and, perching on the arm of his chair, she put her arm round his shoulders. She had never seen her father so subdued. It was as if all the stuffing had been knocked out of him.

'Father, we are not anti-Jew,' said Arthur earnestly, changing his tone.

Jim Blake lifted his head. 'Tell that to the Jews who've had to flee from Adolf Hitler!'

'We would still let them come into Britain. Yes, we would!'

'On certain conditions.'

'Surely that is fair enough?'

'Well, of course, depends what you think is fair. You would never give them full citizenship. Or equal rights.'

'Immigrants shouldn't expect to have the same privileges. Why should they? After all, this is *our* country. Look at how many Irish are living along our street! What about the Flynns? What good are they to us? They didn't come here for our benefit. But for their's!'

Isabella restrained herself. She mustn't open her mouth even though she found it hard to keep quiet. She longed to yell – *scream* – at Arthur. But this was between Arthur and his father.

By now the fire had returned to their father. He was on his feet now and facing his son full on. 'You have been corrupted, Arthur,' he said in a carefully moderated voice, 'and while you hold on to these beliefs that I find totally abhorrent I cannot allow you to remain under my roof. I am sorry to have to say this but I *cannot.*'

'I shall go then!' Arthur showed no emotion.

'Very well,' said his father.

Arthur turned on his heel, left the room and went quickly up the stairs. No more than five minutes later they heard him coming back down, opening the front door and leaving the house.

'He'll go and live in the Black House in Chelsea,' said Isabella.

'So be it,' said her father.

Twenty two

On Saturday afternoon Isabella slipped out of the house saying she was going for a walk. She went only a short distance on foot, then hopped on a bus going downtown, changed on to another, walked a fair distance, and finally arrived in the Kings Road. Chelsea was a long way from Mile End.

She slowed her steps now. What was she doing here? She wasn't sure, she had acted on impulse, almost without thinking. Ever since the row and his hasty departure, she wanted to confront Arthur but what good would it do? He wouldn't listen to her.

Some way ahead, coming towards her, were four young women. They were walking in tight formation, taking up most of the pavement. They were dressed in black and wore black forage caps, their armbands sporting the symbol of the Blackshirts, the one she had seen in Arthur's drawer. A white flash inside a blue circle on a red foreground. They walked with vigour and confidence, their heads held high, arms swinging, shoulders back, as if it was their right to occupy the entire pavement. Like soldiers on parade, they kept in step with each other. Isabella had never thought about women actually being Blackshirts. Their faces glowed. As they came nearer she could hear they were singing. It sounded to Isabella like a marching song. She caught occasional phrases on the wind.

Join in our song . . .

March in spirit with us . . .

She moved into the side. They passed her without a glance but as they did she caught the rest of their song.

And urge on us on to gain the Fascist state.

A *Fascist* state! The very word made her father's blood boil.

'Good afternoon, Miss Isabella,' said a voice behind her.

She wheeled around to see Rupert standing there, legs astride, arms wide open, as if to block her way. He was wearing grey trousers and a loose-belted, black fencing tunic, and he had the usual smile on his face. Isabella imagined him getting up in the morning, admiring himself in the mirror and putting on the smile, like a mask.

'Well, well,' he said, 'so you couldn't stay away! Were you admiring those young ladies who just passed you? I saw you looking at them. Handsome, aren't they? And they're excellent athletes. They know how to keep themselves fit.' He abandoned his pose to come closer to her. 'Were you hoping to see Arthur? You don't have to worry about him, you know. You can take my word for it.'

She wouldn't take his word for anything!

'He hasn't sold his soul to the devil,' added Rupert.

'You have twisted my brother's head,' said Isabella.

'Oh no, you're wrong! You underestimate him.'

Did she? she asked herself. Perhaps she had. He had always been obstinate as a child and had wanted to go his own way.

'I think your brother has a mind of his own,' said Rupert. 'He saw the light for himself. He cares about his country.'

Isabella did not respond. She was trying to think back to their childhood. Arthur had always been very patriotic, and there was nothing wrong with that, as her father said, but she seemed to remember him making remarks about Jews and black people from when he was quite small. A number of their neighbours did as a matter of course without thinking anything of it and they'd add, when speaking to Isabella's mother, 'Oh, not you, Mrs Blake. You might be furren but you're a lady. Anyone can see that. And you've got such a lovely husband, a real English gent.'

Sean, Isabella knew, had often been taunted at school, called a Paddie or a Mick amongst other things, but he'd been able to stand up for himself and had dished out more than one black eye, just as his brothers had. The taunters had soon learned to leave the Flynn family alone.

'Why don't you let me buy you a cup of tea, Isabella?' Rupert asked softly. 'You look tired.' He put his hand under her elbow and led her off down the street. To her surprise she let him take her. She felt exhausted, almost drained of energy.

They went to the same café as before.

'Why don't you take your coat off?' suggested Rupert. 'You'd be more comfortable without it.' He was already helping to ease it over her shoulders. She felt listless and powerless to resist.

'Shall I hang it up for you, sir?' asked the waitress.

'Please, if you would, Beryl.'

'My pleasure, sir.'

Isabella's coat was borne off by Beryl into the nether regions of the café. They sat down. Rupert ordered tea and cakes. Did he bring other girls here to sweeten them up? Beryl called him 'sir' at every opportunity and bobbed around, almost in a curtsey. In return, he was exceedingly civil to her and rewarded her with a smile each time she brought something to the table.

After Isabella had drunk her first cup of tea she felt herself stirring back into life. She accepted a cake when

Rupert held out the plate. She felt as if she needed something sweet.

'You seem interested in our organisation?' said Rupert. She shrugged.

'Why don't you just admit it? Wouldn't you like to come along to one of our events, just to see for yourself? A social? Be introduced to some of our young ladies. I'm sure you would enjoy their company. What about it?'

'Don't think so.' She avoided his eyes, which were trying to connect with hers.

'What are you scared of, Isabella?'

'Nothing.' She shrugged. And then to shift the subject away from herself asked, 'You seem to have managed to recruit Madge. Is she going to be a Blackshirt?'

He laughed. 'Madge?' he said with a derisive laugh. 'I hardly think so!'

'Why, what's wrong with her? Isn't she good-looking enough for you?'

He made a face. 'She's pretty in a flimsy sort of way. Soft, I suppose you could say. She wouldn't stick it. Now you are not soft!'

Isabella felt her face heating up. She glanced down at her plate and the half-eaten cream cake which she no longer wanted. Why had she been so stupid as to come here? Why hadn't she learned from the last time? Curiosity killed the cat, they said.

'She could be firmed up of course,' said Rupert.

Isabella looked up. 'Madge?'

'Who else? Her little friends too.'

'*Firmed up*?' Isabella frowned. 'In what way?'

'For a start, physical exercises can do a lot. Tones the muscles and the mind too.'

Isabella could not imagine Madge doing exercises in a gymnasium or playing rounders in a field.

'But her main problem is that she's not very intelligent,' continued Rupert. 'She's got a sloppy mind. She can't concentrate for more than two minutes whereas you –'

Isabella broke in on him, no longer afraid to look him straight in the eye. 'Yet you encourage her!' she said indignantly. 'She thinks you really like her!'

'I like her well enough.'

'Well enough? Well enough to hand out leaflets. To chat people up. You use her.'

'I like it when you're angry. You look very pretty with those dark eyes flashing. You have a strong backbone – I like that. You would make a good Blackshirt girl.'

She glared at him. 'I am part gypsy, did you know that?'

'As a matter of fact, Madge told me.'

'She would!'

'But you don't live like a gypsy. Or think like a gypsy.'

'How do you know I don't?'

'It's obvious! All right, you dance flamenco and you

dance it exceedingly well. But you are English. You belong here. Don't deny it!'

'Part of me belongs to Spain. It's in my blood.'

'You may like to think so –'

'I *feel* it!'

He shrugged. 'That's a romantic idea. But people change.'

'Or can be changed?'

'Of course!'

She had had enough of this conversation. 'I must go,' she said, pushing back her chair and getting to her feet. 'Thank you for the tea.'

'Come on now, Isabella,' he said, changing gear, turning on his soft, sinuous voice, 'you don't have to go. Why don't you sit down, finish your cake and have another cup of tea?'

'Because I don't want to.'

'Hang on a moment.' He snapped his fingers at the waitress and called for the bill. 'I'll give you a lift home on my motorbike,' he said, adding, 'It's new, it goes like a treat.'

In a flash, Isabella asked, 'Made in Germany?'

'Why, yes, as a matter of fact it was. The Germans make excellent cars and motorbikes.'

'I am going home by bus, thank you.'

It was now that Isabella realised she'd made a mistake by surrendering her coat. She couldn't make a quick escape. She'd had no option but to let him take off her coat. Or had she? She could have insisted, couldn't she, even though he'd taken her by surprise? She was not sure where exactly her coat might have been put. She looked around for help. Beryl had gone to the desk to fetch their bill while another waitress was serving a large party.

Beryl brought the bill and Rupert settled it straight away, leaving a large tip. Beryl did one of her half-curtseys. 'Thank you, sir. Thank you ever so much.'

'That's all right, Beryl.' He patted her arm, making her blush. 'You deserve it. You give excellent service.'

Isabella waited for a chance to break in. 'Excuse me,' she began, but Rupert quickly interceded.

'Wait there, Isabella. I'll fetch your coat for you.'

He went off through to the back of the café.

'He's a real gentleman, ain't he?' said the waitress, gazing after him. 'Ever so handsome and such lovely manners.'

Isabella did not reply. She was fuming. She was furious with him, but even more furious with herself for being so stupid as to let him manipulate her.

Rupert came back with her coat and held it out for her to put on. To refuse his help would draw too much attention to them. She didn't want to make a scene in the middle of the floor with everybody looking on.

'Thank you again, Beryl,' Rupert called as they were

ready to leave. He had his hand under Isabella's elbow, steering her towards the door. 'We'll see you soon.'

We will do nothing of the sort, thought Isabella as she shook off his hand and went striding on ahead of him.

Outside she began to run and so did he, more than able to keep up with her. He jogged along comfortably. The pavements were busy with Saturday shoppers. They had to dodge in and out of the crowd.

Isabella finally came to an abrupt halt and spun round to face him. 'Why can't you just leave me alone!'

'You attract me, Isabella. You attract me very much indeed. I love your fire.'

Without giving it any thought she raised her hand and slapped him hard across the cheek. Heads turned to watch. Two women giggled.

'That's right, dear,' called out one of them. 'Let 'im have it!'

Rupert had covered his flaming cheek with his hand. He stared at her with hard, cold eyes.

She had humiliated him.

He would never forgive her.

Twenty three

Isabella felt shaken all the way home on the bus. The look Rupert had given her had been one of sheer hatred.

She met her dad coming along the road. He had been at a football match.

'What's up with you?' he asked, taking her arm and turning to look into her face. 'Has something happened?'

She shook her head.

'Tell me!'

She didn't want to worry him but she needed to talk to somebody and that person couldn't be Sean. His temper would spill over and he'd head straight for Chelsea, with fists clenched at the ready. Anyway, she'd always confided in her dad.

'Come on, love,' he said, 'let's go for a walk and you can tell me all about it. I don't think you're ready to go home yet. I know your mother! She can smell trouble a mile off.'

Isabella couldn't stop herself blurting out the whole story.

Her father shook his head. 'What on earth made you go to a café with a man like that?' he asked.

'I don't know. But I did. I'm worried, Dad, in case he comes over here.'

'He won't,' said her dad reassuringly. 'He must know he'd meet strong opposition if he did.' For a start the Flynns would be out in force if they scented Blackshirts on their territory.

'He could bring a whole gang of Blackshirts with him,' said Isabella.

'I don't think so somehow. I doubt if they're up for street fighting. They're more sophisticated than that. And do you think this fellow Rupert is actually going to admit to his mates that a *girl* slapped his face? He'd feel humiliated.'

Isabella nodded. Perhaps her dad was right. Rupert was too proud to let himself be seen as a loser.

'There's Arthur . . .' she began.

'Your brother can take care of himself. There'd be no point in Rupert taking it out on him. He's already won Arthur over to his camp.' Her father spoke with sadness and Isabella realised just what a huge blow Arthur's defection had been to him. She squeezed his arm. He'd lost one son to the Fascists, who might have killed his other one. She shivered.

'Are you all right now?' asked her dad. 'Don't worry too much about Rupert. He'll stay clear of here. He'd be a fool if he didn't.'

Isabella felt somewhat reassured, though not totally. She couldn't forget the vicious look on Rupert's face.

Sean called for her in the evening. She was in the scullery washing the dishes.

'On you go, dear,' said her mother. 'I will finish off here. Your father will dry for me. He is good man. I hope you help your mother, Sean?'

Sean looked sheepish. 'A bit. I bring in the coal and I clear out the ashes.'

'I'm glad.' Maria Blake was fond of Sean.

'I've got a bit of money, Issie,' he said once they were outside. 'I earned a few extra bob helping Kenny Jones out this afternoon.' Kenny was a local builder, small time. 'I thought we might go into the West End. I'll treat you in a good café.'

But Isabella was reluctant to stray too far from home in case she encountered Rupert. 'I'd be just as happy to go to Stevie's place.'

'We can go there any old time.'

'I don't mind. Anyway, wouldn't Bridie want to come? She'll be on her own.'

'I never seem to get you on your own these days,' complained Sean. 'Let's go for a walk.'

The streets were still busy, it being a mild spring evening. They headed for the park.

It was unlikely Rupert would make his way over to Hackney and Victoria Park. Isabella couldn't get him out of her mind. She couldn't believe he would let things rest as they were.

There were still families out in the park, taking advantage of the lighter evenings. Some were playing rounders, two girls were playing leapfrog, while others rode the merry-go-round or just idled about. It all looked very peaceful and a million miles from the BUF barracks. Isabella relaxed. They wandered over to a quiet part.

'Why don't we sit down?' suggested Sean. 'The grass is good and dry, so it is.'

He was right. Isabella lay back, resting on her elbows.

'I've a wee ting I'm wantin' to ask you,' said Sean awkwardly

His speech had suddenly become more Irish, which it did when he was nervous. At school he and his brothers had always had their accents pointed out by teachers, who encouraged them to speak properly, that is, in English. They spoke a mixture of accents now.

Isabella was on the alert. What could it be for Sean to sound so serious?

'You're my girl, aren't you?' he asked in a rush.

'How'd you mean?' she asked, though she understood well enough. It was the 'my' that bothered her.

'Well, we're special together. I was thinkin' we might get engaged in a year or so . . .'

'*Engaged*?' Isabella was stunned. Get engaged? To be *married*? She'd always thought that in a vague way that she'd probably get married sometime, like most girls, but the idea of actually getting engaged, tied down, had never entered her head. She and Bridie had often fantasised about getting married, especially when they'd been to the pictures. Imagine marrying Clarke Gable or Cary Grant! It was that kind of chatter.

'We're too young, Sean,' she said, 'to be thinking of –'

He cut across her. 'You'll be sixteen next year. Me mam was only sixteen when she got engaged to me dad. He was eighteen. They got married the year after.'

Isabella thought about his mother. She'd had eight children, two of whom had died at birth. Mrs Flynn wasn't quite forty, yet she looked nearer sixty.

'You like me, don't you, Issie? *Really* like me?'

She nodded. 'Course I do.'

'That's all right then.' He put his arm round her shoulder.

For a while they didn't speak, then Isabella said, 'I'm thinking of going to night school. To study for Matric.'

'That's all right,' he said uncertainly.

'After that I might go to college and do teacher training. I've been talking about it to my dad. He says there's no reason why I shouldn't.' Except for money, but her dad

222

had said there would be a way to manage and Isabella could work in the holidays and on Saturdays.

Sean was looking less comfortable now, as if he realised that this might be something that could come between them. The evening seemed to have turned chilly. Isabella shivered. They were silent for a while, neither knowing what to say.

'Shall we go to Stevie's?' she suggested.

'If you want.'

She took Sean's hand and tried to start a conversation about going to the pictures one evening the following week, but he did not respond.

There were only two people in the café. Stevie was behind the counter reading a pigeon-racing paper.

'What you havin' then?' asked Stevie, lowering his paper.

Isabella opted for cocoa, Sean for a cup of tea. They sat by the steamed-up window. Sean looked glum.

'Sean,' said Isabella quietly, 'I like you, you know I do.'

'Do I?'

'But we don't need to be thinking ahead.'

He concentrated on stirring his tea.

'We don't know what's going to happen,' she went on. 'In the future, like,' she added awkwardly.

Somebody was shouting outside. Isabella was grateful

223

for the diversion. They cleared a space on the window to see a boy lying on his back on the ground with PC MacDade standing beside him, one booted foot on his stomach. Another constable was coming along the street at a lumbering trot.

'For crying out loud,' said Sean, jumping up. 'Not our Mickey again!' He went rushing out of the café.

'Looks like Mickey's copped it this time,' said Stevie, coming over to the window to get a better view. 'They won't let him get away with it any more, whatever he's been up to. He's been asking for it. Talk about light-fingered! He tried to steal a florin out me till one day, bold as brass, under me nose. But I caught him and gave him such a walloping to make sure he'd never dare show his nose in here again.'

Isabella went out to join Sean. PC MacDade removed his foot from Mickey's stomach. 'Right then, Mickey, up you get and on your dying feet! And give me the fags you've got tucked inside your jacket.' He reached down and took them. Two packets of Woodbines. 'We're goin' for a walk to the station. It'll be the juvenile court for you this time, my lad.'

Sean seized his brother by the collar and dragged him up on to his feet. 'You stupid idiot!' he shouted.

'All right then, Sean, you lay off and leave him to me,' said the constable. 'We'll just put the cuffs on him to make sure we have no more nonsense. He's as slippery as an eel, this lad. You can accompany us to the station if you want, Sean.' He turned to speak to the other constable. 'I'll leave you to call in at the Flynns' house, Albert, and inform his father. You know where they live, don't you?'

'Who doesn't?'

Isabella accompanied the constable along the road.

'What are the chances of Paddy Flynn being sober?' he asked.

Isabella shrugged.

Mrs Flynn, hair ridged with the usual steel curlers, was in her regular position in the doorway talking to another woman. At the sight of Isabella and the policeman she removed the cigarette butt from the corner of her mouth and tossed it into the gutter.

'What's goin' on, Issie? Where's Sean?' she asked anxiously. 'Nothin's happened to him, has it?'

'He's all right, Mrs Flynn,' said the policeman. 'It's your youngest that isn't.'

'Not again,' she moaned. 'I don't know what to be doin' with him, Constable. But you won't be hard on him, will you? He's a decent boy at heart. There's nothin' nasty about him.'

'A spell away from home might sort him out.'

'Please no, Constable! I'll give him what for when he comes home.'

'Doubt if that'd do any good. Is your husband in, Mrs Flynn?'

'He just went out a wee while back.'

'To get a breath of fresh air no doubt. It's all right, you don't need to tell me where to find him.'

'What is it, Mum?' Bridie appeared behind her mother in the doorway. Her forehead looked damp with sweat.

'It's our Mickey.'

'Oh no!'

'I'll go and see if I can find your man then, Mrs Flynn,' said the constable, taking his leave.

Isabella went in to talk to Bridie for a little while in the back kitchen. The draining board was piled high with wet clothes.

'I was just trying to wash a few things.' Bridie wiped her forehead with her forearm. 'I'm having to wring them out by hand. Our mangle's broken.'

'You could come along and use ours,' said Isabella. Her mother took most of their washing to the laundry. 'You've got far too much to do now you're working all day. It's not right. Couldn't your mother do a bit more?'

'She's not very well. I worry about her, Issie. You should hear her coughing in the night! Her lungs are in a bad way and she won't go to the doctor.'

They had always shared their secrets, Isabella and Bridie. Isabella considered for a moment, then told her about Rupert.

Bridie promised not to tell anyone, especially Sean, but she was concerned. 'He sounds a nasty one, that Mr Smooth. Stay well away from him, Issie!'

'Don't worry I will. And I'm going to put him out of my head.'

As Isabella was settling down in bed she thought of what Sean had talked about, but only briefly. She was too tired for any more thinking. She fell asleep straight away, glad to shut out all the upsets of the day.

She was jolted awake only an hour or two later. She sat bolt upright. There was a terrible racket going on somewhere outside. Not in the street, from what she could tell. She jumped out of bed and ran into the hall to bump into her father coming running down the stairs in his pyjamas.

'What is it, Dad?'

'Something going on in our back yard. Sounds like a fight.'

Twenty four

Isabella's father switched on the light above the back door. They could now make out two dark figures wrestling on the ground while two others danced around them trying to get into the fray.

Then came a whoop as one of the two combatants was felled, face down in the dirt.

'Sean!' cried Isabella, running forward. He was sitting on top of his victim, puffing a little from the effort. His brothers Dominic and Kieron stood on guard beside him.

'Turn him round, for God's sake,' shouted Jim Blake. 'Let him breathe.'

Sean rolled the man over. He wore a black balaclava obscuring his face but Isabella knew before it was pulled back who the man would be. Even so she gasped as he stared back at her with eyes full of venom.

'Do you know this man, Isabella?' asked her dad.

'Yes. He's a friend –' she faltered.

'Of *yours*?'

'No, of course not! He's Arthur's friend. He's in the BUF. It's Rupert.'

'He was going to petrol bomb your house, Mr Blake,' cried Sean. 'I'm tellin' you! Look, there's the can over there! He flung it away when I jumped him.'

Dominic went to look and picked up the can. 'The top's off,' he yelled. 'It's spilling petrol all over the place.'

They could smell it.

'Get water,' cried Jim Blake, heading back to the house. 'Quickly! And nobody drop a fag or a match.'

'What happens, Jim?' asked his wife, appearing in the doorway in her dressing gown.

'Stay inside, love. Dominic, go for the police! Tell them it's urgent!'

By now Fergal, Sean's eldest brother, had also arrived and the neighbours on both sides of the Blakes were hanging over their walls. Mr Mann jumped over to offer his help, landing rather heavily on one foot. He was a portly man and not very agile. Isabella hoped he hadn't sprained his ankle.

In the next few minutes she and her parents filled every receptacle they had – pots, pans, basins – with water and soaked the ground. Isabella soaked her pyjamas too.

The police arrived in a van, four of them, and came charging through the house with their batons drawn. Sean got up and released Rupert into their care. He was forced on to his feet and led away in handcuffs. He didn't utter a single word but he turned to give Isabella one last look, which made her shiver.

'Don't worry about him,' said her dad. 'He'll be behind bars for the next few years. He'll be charged with arson and attempted murder. We had a lucky escape, thanks to Sean. He saved our lives.'

Isabella nodded. Sean had been very brave. He might have had the can of petrol poured over him. She would never have imagined Rupert being a petrol bomber. It didn't fit with his cool, controlled exterior. She said so next day when she was talking it over with her father.

'But you obviously enraged him,' he said, 'and when people fly into a rage they are capable of doing all manner of things they might otherwise not do. Especially when they think they are invincible.'

'Dad,' said Isabella, smiling, 'you should have gone to college yourself, you put things so well.'

'It just wasn't possible,' he replied without any rancour. 'But for you . . .?'

She nodded.

The following evening, while they were eating, there was a knock on the door. Usually the caller would put his head round the door and shout out. But not this time. Isabella went to see who it was. A man, tall, well dressed in a dark suit and wearing a bowler hat, stood there, leaning on a silver-topped stick. A taxi was pulling away from the kerb.

'Good evening,' he said, tipping his hat. 'I hope I haven't called at an inconvenient moment?'

'Well,' Isabella began. He must surely be aware of the strong smell of mutton stew that had followed her to the door.

'Who is it, Issie?' asked her father, coming to join her.

'Mr Blake?' The visitor lifted his hat again. 'Mr Anderson at your service, sir.'

'You're Angus's dad?' cried Isabella.

He bowed his head in acknowledgement. 'Exactly so.'

'Please do come in, Mr Anderson,' said Isabella's dad, holding out his hand. 'I'm Jim Blake.'

Mr Anderson took the extended hand and removed his hat altogether. They moved into the lobby. Isabella could hear her mother scurrying about in the living room, trying to tidy up.

'And this is my daughter, Isabella,' said her father.

'Ah yes,' said Mr Anderson, shaking hands with her, 'I gathered it must be. I have heard about you.'

'So you have seen Angus?' said Jim Blake. He held open the living-room door and invited Mr Anderson to go in.

'I have just come from the hospital,' he said.

Isabella's mother had managed to clear away some of the dishes from the table, though a number remained.

Her jet-black hair, normally worn neatly coiled on top of her head, had come adrift from its scarlet comb, and was tumbling down around her shoulders.

Her husband introduced her to their visitor and they shook hands, after she had wiped hers on the corner of her apron.

'I am sorry, not very tidy –' she began, but he interrupted.

'The apology is all mine, madam. I have come at an inconvenient moment. I shall not detain you for long.'

Isabella hovered anxiously, keen to find out how the meeting between Angus and his father had gone. Finally, Mr Anderson was seated, having turned down the offer of a cup of tea or a glass of port or sherry. He was fine, he said, he required nothing. He had partaken of afternoon tea at his club.

Isabella wondered why he would have a club in London when he lived in Scotland? He didn't have much of a Scottish accent, she noticed, unlike Robbie.

As if he had read her mind Mr Anderson said, 'I find it useful to have a club in London when I come to do business in the city. I shall pass the night there.'

'So,' said Jim Blake, 'how did you find Angus?'

'In a sorry state.' Mr Anderson shook his head. 'I am going to take him back to Edinburgh with me. I have booked a first-class sleeper on the night train from King's Cross Station for tomorrow.'

'That's good.' Jim Blake nodded. 'I am glad you are reunited.'

Mr Anderson did not reply to that. He said, 'You were very kind taking him in as you did and I would like to recompense you.' He pulled out a leather wallet.

Jim Blake held up a hand. 'We do not need to be recompensed. We didn't do it for that reason.'

Mr Anderson held out several notes. 'I insist.'

'And we do not wish to take it,' said Jim Blake equally firmly. 'We are not in need of charity.'

There was a pause and then Angus's father laid the notes on a side table and stood up. Isabella wondered what would happen now. Her father was too dignified to start slinging pound notes around while Mr Anderson, she felt sure, was used to getting his own way.

Her father looked at the money and said, 'Very well. We shall put it in the Poor Box in the local church.'

'Do as you wish,' said Angus's father. He nodded in the direction of Isabella and her mother. 'I will take my leave then, and thank you again. I don't suppose you could call me a taxi?'

'We have no phone,' replied Jim Blake. 'There's a public call box in the next street or you might be lucky and pick up a cab, though not very many come this way.'

'It was starting to drizzle when I came in and I, unfortunately, left my umbrella in the club.' Mr Anderson glanced in Isabella's direction. Was he going to ask her to run out and look for a taxi for him? If he had been, he changed his mind.

Jim Blake saw him out. When he came back he announced, 'Unfortunately the drizzle has turned to rain.'

They couldn't help laughing.

'Poor Angus,' said Isabella. 'I'll go and see him on my way home from work tomorrow.'

Angus was sitting up against a pile of pillows. His eyes looked brighter and his face was a better colour than she'd ever seen it.

'Did my father call?' he asked straight away.

Isabella nodded and pulled up a chair to the bed.

'What did you think of him?' asked Angus.

She shrugged. 'He was only in for a few minutes.'

'You can be honest with me. So tell me!'

'He's not a very warm man.'

Angus burst out laughing. 'Warm? He's like an icicle!'

'But you're going home with him?'

'I can't stay here, can I? I won't live with him for long though. My uncle will take me in. He's my father's brother and a lawyer too but they're like chalk and cheese.'

'Like my two brothers. What will you do when you get home?'

'Go to university. In the autumn.'

'To become a lawyer?'

'No, I've decided to study medicine. Perhaps being here . . .' He glanced round the ward.

Isabella told Angus about Rupert and his attempt to burn down their house.

'That's terrible!' exclaimed Angus. 'To think you could have died! It doesn't bear thinking of.' He reached out and took her hand.

Isabella stayed with him right through visiting time. He talked a bit more about the war in Spain than he had before, about seeing so many of his friends being mown down, collapsing in the mud. Isabella thought of William and her throat dried.

'Isabella, he may still come back,' said Angus quietly. 'Don't give up hope. The wounded were being taken off to all sorts of different places to recover.'

The bell rang for the end of visiting hour. Isabella was reluctant to leave and he was reluctant to let go of her hand.

'I'll write to you, Isabella. Will you write back? Promise?'

She promised.

'Come closer,' he said. She did and then he kissed her. 'I'll turn up at your door one of these days, Isabella,' he said. 'Would you like me to?'

She nodded.

'And perhaps sometime we might go somewhere special together. Like Paris?'

'I'd love to go to Paris!'

'I'll take you!'

She had never spent a night away from their house except for the holiday in Spain. They couldn't afford to go away on holidays. In summer they went on day trips to Southend on Sea and as far as Brighton a couple of times. They had been good days but they could not match up to the promise of Paris. *Paris.* Was it possible that she would actually be able to go there and see the Eiffel Tower and walk down the wide boulevards? She had read about the city in an illustrated book she'd borrowed from the library.

'Kiss me again,' said Angus.

The matron was advancing up the ward towards them with a determined stride. 'All visitors must leave *immediately*!'

Isabella looked back from the doorway to wave to Angus. He blew her a kiss in return.

She walked home in a kind of dream. *He will come,* she thought, *one of these days.*

She was so far away in her head that at first she did not see the figure at the door. And when she did she barely recognised him. He was a like a ghost of the brother she had known.

'William!' she cried.

Twenty five

The rejoicing in the street at William's return was so great that the Blakes decided to hold a party. They borrowed trestle tables from two church halls and set them up end to end down the middle of the road. Everyone brought as much food and drink as they could afford. The tables were heaped high. William's father provided flagons of cider and bottles of beer and his mother spent a day baking cinnamon biscuits and custard tarts. Isabella, aided by Bridie, made doughnuts with strawberry jam in the middle and dusted them with icing sugar on the outside. They'd always been William's favourites. The butcher contributed two dozen mutton pies and the baker an enormous white iced sponge cake with WELCOME HOME WILLIAM emblazoned on the top in thick chocolate letters.

The proceedings began with Jim Blake banging on the table with a gavel lent by a local auctioneer. Everyone fell silent except for Mrs Flynn, who had been too busy gossiping to pay attention. Her husband, sober, though not for long, hit her in the back. She gave him a filthy look in return but quietened.

Jim Blake stood up to speak. He cleared his throat. He thanked everyone for coming and for their support during the last difficult months.

'You can imagine how happy we are to have our dear William returned to us,' he began, his voice creaking with emotion.

Loud cheers erupted right along the row of tables. William had always been a popular boy, ready to give a helping hand to anyone who needed it. His mother smiled through her tears.

'We are very proud of him,' continued Jim Blake, to more cheers and banging of spoons on table tops. 'So let us drink to William!'

'To William!'

They stood to drink the toast. William remained seated, his thin face flushed. He raised his left arm in acknowledgement. His right one was missing, blown away by a blast of machine-gun fire in a foreign field.

So the revellers eat and drink and soon a singsong starts up.

My old man said 'Follow the van
and don't dilly dally on the way . . .'

Bridie sits close to William, helping him, watching

238

over him. She will look after him, thinks Isabella, and one day they will marry. Mickey sits next his mother looking as if butter wouldn't melt in his mouth. He has been put on probation and signs in at the police station daily. His mother gave him a good telling-off but no one has much faith in that having any effect on Mickey.

Isabella sits beside her good friend Sean. His arm rests lightly across her shoulders. He is relaxed. Rupert is behind bars and Angus has gone back to Scotland.

Isabella's brother Arthur is here too. After Rupert's failed attempt to burn down their house he came home to mutter his apologies. He has left the BUF. They could tell he was deeply ashamed. He sits at the table now amongst his family but he looks brooding and far away in his head. Isabella does not know what he will do now.

All thoughts of Adolf Hitler warmongering in Europe and Franco laying waste in Spain are far from their minds on such a day. Summer is coming, the buds are out on the trees, and William is home. They have something to celebrate.

To find out more about Joan Lingard and
discover other exciting books, visit:

www.catnippublishing.co.uk